T0006112

NO LOVE CITY

HUGH ROGERS

NO LOVE CITY

Copyright © 2022 Hugh Rogers.

All rights reserved. No part of this book may be used or reproduced by any means, graphic, electronic, or mechanical, including photocopying, recording, taping or by any information storage retrieval system without the written permission of the author except in the case of brief quotations embodied in critical articles and reviews.

This is a work of fiction. All of the characters, names, incidents, organizations, and dialogue in this novel are either the products of the author's imagination or are used fictitiously.

iUniverse books may be ordered through booksellers or by contacting:

iUniverse
1663 Liberty Drive
Bloomington, IN 47403
www.iuniverse.com
844-349-9409

Because of the dynamic nature of the Internet, any web addresses or links contained in this book may have changed since publication and may no longer be valid. The views expressed in this work are solely those of the author and do not necessarily reflect the views of the publisher, and the publisher hereby disclaims any responsibility for them.

Any people depicted in stock imagery provided by Getty Images are models, and such images are being used for illustrative purposes only. Certain stock imagery © Getty Images.

ISBN: 978-1-6632-2483-5 (sc)
ISBN: 978-1-6632-2484-2 (e)

Library of Congress Control Number: 2022902147

Print information available on the last page.

iUniverse rev. date: 05/11/2022

ACKNOWLEDGEMENTS

First and foremost, I want to thank my Lord and Savior Jesus Christ. All things were created by him and for him; and he is before all things, and by him all things consist of.

To my mother Dorothy Butler, and grandmother Mattie B. Benjamin, thank you for always believing in me. For always speaking to the man you knew I could be, the man God created me to be. You never gave up on me. Even when I was messing up, your unconditional love guided me through, ass whippings followed by hugs.

To my beautiful wife Terry, your demonstration of love has given me the courage to love without limit nor fear. You came into my life at a time when I was at my lowest and lifted me. You are my motivation to achieve greater, your love is my driving force to chase and capture my dreams.

To my children, "May the life ahead of you keep your capacity for faith and belief, but let your judgement watch what you believe, keep your love of life, but throw away your fear of death. Life must be loved, or it is lost…keep your wonder at great and noble things, like sunlight and thunder, the rain and the stars, and greatness of heroes. Keep your heart hungry for new knowledge. Keep your hatred for a lie and keep your power of indignation…" (a letter from a Yugoslav soldier in World War II before he was executed.)

To my siblings, as the quote unquote baby of the babies, I received from you, all the love and support needed to believe in a better day in a world as cold as the one we live in. Thank you for that and I love y'all right back.

In the words of the legendary Tupac Amaru Shakur; "To all my homies that I used to have that no longer rolled, catch a brother at the crossroads." Our paths in this life were already selected long before they ever connected. I ain't mad at none of y'all, live strong and I pray long my brothas.

Finally, to all my peeps who think I forgot about you, I could never do that, it's just so many of y'all and so little space.

This book is dedicated to my mother Dorothy L. Butler

There's not a day that goes by that I don't wish you were here. I know that right now you're probably looking down on me smiling saying that's my baby followed by words of encouragement like you've always given to me. Thank you mama, I love you with all that I am forever.

Big Ardelle

CHAPTER 1

THE CREW

Spring 1991

"YO MAMA SO dumb the weatherman said it was gonna be chilly outside this morning, and she ran and got a bowl. Talking 'bout, 'Baby, you can take some of that for lunch today!'" Phil said, cracking on Troy as Rick and Bang busted up laughing.

"Oh, so y'all think that shit funny, huh? Bang, y'all so poor that, when I came to ya house for Thanksgiving, yo mama was boiling a bone. And, Rick, yo fat ass mama jumped up in the air and got stuck!"

"Yeah, yeah, yeah," Rick said. "Keep that shit between you two niggas. Don't be tryna put us up in that shit cuz he is roasting that ass."

"Yeah!" Phil said. "Rick's moms ain't fat; she thick! Everybody knows Vicki's thick with dat big ole booty!"

"Dayum!" Bang and Troy hollered as the 8:30 bell rang. This was an everyday thing for the Crew, cracking jokes on each other and all who were around them each morning before school. Then they'd head over to Troy's house afterward to play Sega Genesis, where the joke cracking continued for the rest of the day. Troy's house was the kick it spot, because his mother's approach to raising boys was very laid-back.

Troy's older brother was the coolest dude they knew at thirteen and fourteen years old. He had a crew of his own, and he was their leader. It seemed like Troy always had the newest things out, from shoes to video games because of his older brother. When Troy was nine, he had a quarter with a hole drilled through it and a string attached so that he could slip it into the video games at the game room and then snatch it back out as soon as the credits registered. The Crew played games for free that entire summer—up until the owner, Mr. Bryant, caught Bang using it. Troy always had the scams for the Crew to get over because his brother was pretty much into everything, which was, no doubt, why he ended up going to jail.

"Yo, what time is Thicky Vicki coming home tonight?" Phil asked.

Rick, always on guard, replied, "Nigga what time is Effie fat ass coming to the crib tonight?" still working the game controller.

"Sissy booty ass nigga, I asked cuz Troy found his brother's fuck flicks stash. But yo ole scary ass ain't tryna see no pussy—probably scared to death, ole coo ass nigga!"

"Nigga, fuck you! She 'on' get home till like around eleven, so it's whateva. And for the record, nigga, I ain't no coo! You 'on' even know what the fuck a coo is. You just tryna sound like Troy brotha n'em."

"You 'on' even know what a coo is. You just tryna sound like Troy brotha n'em!" Phil mimicked him. "Just bring y'all lame asses on!" he said, referring to both Rick and Bang still playing the game as he headed for the door.

"Aye let's walk around to Amanda's crib. I bet Daneshia n'em over there. We gonna see if Troy got the game to get 'em to slide ova to Rick's house to watch this shit with us," Phil suggested.

Troy really did have a way with words when it came to the girls, cuz in no time, he had them convinced to meet them over at Rick's house to watch porn. Eighth grade was the last time they'd all hung out together.

Phil, Troy, and Bang had joined the neighborhood gang by the middle of their freshmen year of high school. They'd dropped out and started hanging on the corner by the liquor store, where drugs were being sold. When Rick's mom noticed they'd taken to hanging there with the gangbangers and drug dealers, they were no longer welcome to step foot across her threshold, and Rick's days of hanging out with them were over. She started making Rick go to church more and kept him busy doing housework when he was home.

"Ricky, go to the store for me. I need some stockings for church tomorrow. And don't be out there stopping on that corner with them fools you call friends. So many people done got shot out there. Them boys ain't on their way nowhere but to hell!"

"Why you 'on' like Phil and n'em no more, Mama?"

"It's not that I don't like them, baby. I don't like the things they're into, and I just want better for you. That fast life they're tryna to live ain't nothing but a fast trip to jail or the grave. And Satan the devil is a lie if he thinks he's gonna have you. As for me and my household, we shall serve the Lord! Now here. And get me some washing powder and Hills Bros. coffee too."

Rick hated not being able to hang out with the Crew. He knew what they were doing out there slanging and banging, but he had absolutely no interest in any of that. He hated drugs for what they had done to his aunt Vienne and what they'd made her do to get her next fix. He remembered how bad his aunt had looked in the hospital before she'd died. She was a heroin addict and had contracted AIDS from sharing needles with her dope-shooting friends. But before that, she had been his favorite auntie, who'd always wanted him to dance for her and with her. She'd bought him anything he wanted whenever she came around. Her boyfriend, Earl, got strung out first. And it wasn't long before she was too. Rick never liked drugs after that and vowed never to use or sell them.

"What's up wit' it, Rick?" Bang said as Rick approached him, standing by the corner store.

"Nothing, what's up with you, stud? Mr. Sheffield told me to tell you the next time I saw you that he thought you were coming back to play for him this year, man. He also said to tell you he can still help you get back in school and that you should really think about it before it's too late." Rick delivered the message from Mr. Sheffield, the basketball coach at Dunbar Vocational High School. Coach was always on them, trying to help them become something more than what was around them. He knew that Kevin, which was Bang's real name, had potential and where it could take him if he'd just get off the streets and back in school.

"Naw, man, I gotta get this money right now, you feel me? That school shit just ain't cutting it for a nigga right now. But anyway, man kid, yo moms be having that ass up in church like every day on some holy shit like you the fuckin' pastor and shit, my nigga. I know you be like, "If this is what it takes to get to heaven, fuck it, just send me to hell, huh, my nigga?" he said with a light chuckle, attempting to change the subject.

"It's cool, you know. A lot of girls be there, and ain't nobody getting shot or shot at like out here on the block either."

"Yeah, and you know what else ain't nobody getting? No money or pussy up in there. No wait, nobody but the preacher!" Bang shot back with another chuckle.

"I heard all that shooting last night. Anybody get smoked out here?"

"Naw, that was me just testing out my new shit—you know, letting them niggas across the tracks know that we got it for they ass ova here whenever they want it."

"Nigga. We call you Bang cuz when you was a baby you were always running into shit, not cuz you was destined to become the next Billy the Kid!" Rick said, and they both shared a laugh.

Bang was rapidly becoming a known gunner in the neighborhood—which meant he'd pull and shoot without a moment's hesitation. His reputation proceeded him, bringing both respect and threats to the name. But to him, the respect was a flattering high, while the threats were beyond his present concerns. One thing was for sure. As the years went by, he lived up to the name, putting in the necessary work and even gaining a few bodies under his belt.

CHAPTER 2

Summer 1996

FOP, FOP, FOP, fop, fop!

"Nigga what!" Lil Polk yelled, spreading his arms after shooting at the passing car with four rival gang members. All with hats cocked to the sides of their heads. "Them muthafuckin tricks gonna stop coming through here like shit sweet!" he said returning the 9mm Glock to his waist.

Tension was always thick between rival gangs in the city, especially during the summer months. But make no mistake, Chicago kept it gangsta all year round. Bodies lay cold in the gutter on top of crimson-colored snow and ice in the winter as well. The theme in the city was get down how you live, and the Crew was down to get it anyway it came—from stickups to carjacking to gambling or hustling—anything that brought a dollar.

Gangbanging was a part of everyday life in the Chi; only on the West Side did different mobs exist on the same block corners, separated only by maybe twenty feet, if that, and they all got money. The South Siders never took to that concept—*nope*! Out south, every gang banged for turf. It was all about the blocks and neighborhoods they could control. And if you got caught on the wrong block in the wrong neighborhood with your hat cocked to the wrong side, they got right up with you, trying to knock that hat, along with your head, off your body.

For the Crew, that neighborhood was called the Dome, and for blocks and blocks there was nothing but Bros, as they called themselves. You couldn't go five blocks in any direction without still being surrounded by the Bros, except for the few blocks where they'd allowed the Vikings to exist on their turf. The Crew had gotten the OK from their chief to set up shop on the last of the blocks controlled by the Bros. It was kind of like the outskirts just before the true outskirts of the Dome on one of the two blocks that divided the Bros turf from the DDs' territory. It was simple. If the Crew could hold it down against the DDs, or the Brahs as they called themselves, and their chief got his cut of the profits, everything was a go. That included both manpower and firepower when needed.

Not to mention, though, the chief felt the Vikings were starting to get a little too much money in the Dome. They were only allowed to be there because they had grown up there and were under the same umbrella as the Bros, connecting the two gangs. With the Crew being just a couple of blocks away from the Vikings' operation, they could snatch up some of their business, and the chief could profit from the situation nicely.

The hypes had been coming through on the regular now, and everything was seeming to go smoothly. A lot of the young Bros came to hang out on the block seeking a come up and the action it promised, being so close to the borderline of the Dome. Everybody was out to make a name for himself. And what better place than on a new strip in the Dome with the Crew.

"Tricky, let me get one for this seven. I'ma bring you all them niggas' customers from across the tracks!" plead a bony smoker.

"Lou Lou, you been coming short every fuckin time you shop. Hell naw. Get the fuck outta here with that short shit! You don't be takin' them niggas over there short money. You come correct every time you shop with them. So don't come running yo lil bony ass over here with that! Fuck outta here!"

"You know you can do it, Tricky. Shit I been shopping with you all damn day and ain't came short one time. I'll bring you the little funky ass three dollars back!"

"I ain't gonna tell you no more, Lou Lou—*Oh shit, slick boys up the one way*!" he shouted as he got in the wind with the rest of the cats hanging on the block, leaving the begging hype and approaching detectives with nothing but dissatisfaction.

———◦◦◦———

"What's up, bro? Everything good?" Phil said as he approached Troy. They shook hands using the special gang shake.

"Yessir, bro. Everything is truly good. What's good with you, my nigga?" Troy replied.

"Where the fuck is everybody at?" Phil inquired.

"Shit'd, that's what I was thinking, I just got out here myself, and everybody was ghost when I came through the block. I bet them lil muthafuckas got into it with them niggas across the tracks and ain't told nobody shit!" Troy suggested.

"That's how niggas be getting caught slipping out here when them niggas come through busting!" Phil vented.

"On everything, bro. That's how that shit be happening foe sho!" Troy said getting hyped up and animated and pounding his fist into his other hand. "The lil niggas be going across the tracks yackin' at them niggas and then coming back over here like ain't shit happened. And don't nobody be on point, cuz they don't know 'bout the shit!" he continued.

"You seen that nigga Bang today, bro?" Phil inquired.

"Naw. Last time I seen that nigga he was 'bout to go through Pretty crib late last night after we took care of that. That nigga lovesick foe that bitch for real, bro, knowing she ain't nothing but a rat!"

"Yeah, that bitch sho nuff a runna; no doubt 'bout that. But you bet not let that trigga-happy ass nigga hear you saying that shit bout her!" Phil warned with a slight chuckle as he passed the blunt.

"Dat nigga don't wanna fuck around. You think Lil Polk put hands and feet on his ass when he ran up on him with that tripping shit cuz that bitch gave him some pussy. I ain't gonna play no games with 'em, bro, on everything!" Troy said in between pulls off the blunt.

"Matter of fact, here this lovesick ass nigga go right here still driving that damn steama he s'posed to got rid of last night. Aye, why the fuck is you still riding round in that hot-ass shit, nigga? You gonna get the fuckin' block and every nigga ova here locked the fuck up!" Phil barked.

"I got this shit, nigga. Chill the fuck out and let me do this!" said an aggravated Bang.

"Naw, nigga, he right. You know what the deal is with that demo. You bogus as hell, bro. You gonna fuck around and get us knocked!" Troy cut in.

"Quit crying, nigga. Don't nobody wanna hear that shit!" Bang retorted as he pulled off again.

"Next time that nigga do some dumbass shit like that, I'ma give his ass one to the leg, my nigga on my mama!" Phil fumed.

Bang was a young killer, but Phil and Troy were just as deadly, with equal body counts in the hood. Bang just had the catchy name and was more flamboyant with everything he did, causing him to stand out. Phil was the mastermind of the three and, therefore, the most dangerous. Bang was his boy, but he was always doing something stupid that jeopardized them all like his brain didn't work.

"Oh yeah, bro. I ran into this nigga I know name Tony up at the Gyros spot last night. He gave me his number and told me to get at him. I think the nigga was spooked or something, cuz some of the lil Bros was up in there tripping with him and shit. The nigga acted like I was Jesus coming to save him, all glad to see me and shit." Troy exaggerated.

"Is that the nigga they call Tee? He supposed to be a black Colombian or something?" Phil asked.

"Yeah, that's the nigga, and he gettin it! His mom's peeps s'posed to had put him on strong, and now he ridin big body Benz having shit his way. He had a bitch with him last night—I bullshit you not—that looked like she was Chilli from TLC."

"Yeah, I heard 'bout that nigga. So that's what money do for ya, huh?" Phil said before throwing down the tiny remains of the blunt they'd just smoked. "So, when you gonna hit him up?" he asked, releasing the smoke from his lungs.

"I 'on' know, bro. I wish we could grab that nigga and make his people run that bag to get his bitch ass back!"

"You know what, bro? I know just how we can get that nigga. Peep game—when we finish this work we got now, you call him to re-up and see how much he'll charge you foe a four and a split. Then we start shopping with the nigga to get him comfortable so we can get close to him. I know he gonna wanna front you something, cuz ain't no nigga tryna break nothing down—not ridin' round this bitch in a big body Benz!" Phil explained.

"Fo sho, bro that's what we on!" Troy said, rubbing his hands together.

The Crew was jack boys, stickup niggas whenever the opportunity presented itself, and didn't care what set a nigga was hollering when it came time to get em. Lately, though, they'd been hustling slinging rocks since the last jack move they'd pulled and found $50,000 in the trunk. After splitting it three ways and doing some shopping and partying, they barely had enough between them to buy an eighth of a kilo. Because they were known for sticking niggas up, there weren't too many of the Bros that were willing to serve them, and the cats that would were just as grimy as they were and had garbage work, they called whoop.

Now with their own block, they'd been copping from an old cat everybody called Head. His work was good, and the price was right for them because he was messing with Phil's auntie. Head was about his business, though, and had a string of killers in his employ just as dangerous and cruddy as the Crew; only they were loyal to him to the death. Phil knew that, if they ever tried to pull it with him, it wouldn't turn out good for the Crew. So, they always came straight up with him when doing business.

"Ah shit, bro. I knew it was something I wanted to tell you!" Troy said with a slight chuckle. "Lil Polk did some kind of karate chop on Tank and knocked him dead asleep! You know Tank fuck with his sister Tiny, right? I guess he s'posed to been hitting on her and shit. Nigga must've thought that Tae kwon do Lil Polk know was fake or a joke or something!" he said, wiping away tears from laughing so hard.

"Yeah, shorty tough with the hands and feet. Shit'd his old man been teaching him that shit since he was like six! Eva see the old man working out? That nigga used to be kicking the ceiling', knocking down walls in the garage!" Phil said, still laughing.

"When dat nigga Tank came to, he was thanking God in Arabic, talkin' 'bout Al-ham-dul-il-lah. Niggas was saying Lil Polk slap-chopped dat nigga so hard he thought God reached down from heaven and hit 'im!" Troy laughed, with tears streaming down his cheeks. "Dat nigga Tank was in his body talking 'bout what he was gonna do to shorty and shit, so the chief told him to leave it alone until later so he could get a clear drawing of what went down."

"Everybody already know the demo. I 'on' know what they thinking. But ain't nobody 'bout to be fuckin' with shorty for protecting his sista. I don't care who Tank s'posed to be to chief, and that's on my mama!" Phil said as he patted his waist where his gun rested.

CHAPTER 3

"WHAT UP, BRAH?" Danny spoke through the phone as he made his rounds to the spots, collecting last night's generous contributions from the fiends of the city.

"I'm at the crib. Where you at 'B'?" Stank said, flipping through the channels whiling lying across the bed.

"Come on out, brah. I'm pulling up in front right now."

Damn, I hate this game! Danny thought to himself—all the hustle and bustle and chances that came with it. Lately he'd found himself wondering how he'd come to feel this way about the game when it had been so good to him. He had the whole Englewood area on lock from 63rd and Damen to 79th and Halsted. Although he was a DD, he had Bros and Vikings for customers. The sound of Stank tapping on the passenger's side window brought him out of deep thought.

"What's the biz, Babyboy?" Danny said pulling away from the curb.

"This mutha was off the chain last night, brah! I ran through them five joints in about two hours! I was hitting you up like crazy but kept getting yo voice mail and shit," Stank said as he rolled a blunt.

"Yeah, I was at the hospital till like 2:30 this morning with Trina. She was having some kind of stomach pains." His tone was contemplative.

"Ain't nothing wrong with the baby, is it?" Stank questioned.

"Naw. They say shorty straight; it was probably just some gas they think. Shit'd I hope that's all it was!" He sighed.

"Man, B, I started to break them five joints down into zones cuz I knew ain't nobody have shit the way niggas was at me!" Stank said with much regret in his voice.

Stank and Danny had been best friends since Stank had come to live with his aunt Brenda when he was just ten years old. Danny lived across the street. His mother, Judy, and Brenda were good friends who partied together on the weekends. When Stank and his younger sister, Tanya, came to live with Brenda, it was only natural that he and Danny would soon become friends the way Judy and Brenda hung out.

When Danny was seventeen years old, he was hit by a city bus and sued both the city of Chicago and the company of the other driver who'd caused the accident. He'd received a settlement when he was nineteen and began hustling and never looked back.

"I see Mankie and Roc was blowing up my phone too. It must've been jumping cuz they know not to be calling my shit like that!" Danny said, sitting at the light and scrolling through his phone's missed call log. "Oh, and Tee called this morning and said the coast guard popped off the shit they were getting yesterday. He says he's gonna be straight sometime today though. I know his peeps gotta be mad as a muthafucka! Look I got like seven of 'em left. I'ma give you five. Take three and do 'em how you want. Have Ray cook up the other two and have Twin n'em put them into sacks for me. Tell them I need at least seventy out of it, nice sizes like always! I'ma put it out there with Mankie and Roc. Give Twin n'em $2,500 a piece for bagging all that shit up for me. And take care of Ray," Danny instructed as he pulled into the drive-through at KFC.

"Don't you s'posed to be hitting the studio tonight?" Stank inquired.

"Yeah, I'm going about seven. I gotta finish up that one song I told you about the other day. Then I gotta get everything mixed down and mastered. I'ma drop you off at the Cutlass by my granny's block. Everything in there."

"Welcome to KFC, may I take your order?" came the voice over the speaker.

"Yeah, give me a three-piece spicy and a large orange," Danny said.

"Make that two!" Stank yelled from the passenger's side.

"Drive around for your total please," the voice responded.

They rode around for a while longer after eating, not talking about much, just listening to the music before Stank broke out and said, "What's up, Dee? Why you so quiet and shit, brah? Is everything good?"

"Yeah everything straight, brah. A nigga just tired and shit, you know? I got the shorty on the way, these thirsty ass niggas out here, and shit you know."

"Man, B, some niggas been tripping with you or something?" Stank cut in.

"Naw, brah. Ain't no muthafuckas been tripping with me, B! You'd know about it, my nigga. I'm just saying niggas out here thirsty, and thirsty niggas is desperate niggas. So they'll do anything to get rid of a real nigga in the way of em getting money. You see what happened to them niggas out west? How you think they got banged by the Feds? That's all-fair game for these grimy ass dudes out here today. Every nigga ain't going by the code, and every nigga ain't got the heart to come at you and move you outta the way. So they put them people on you. Shit, Stank, you know these niggas out here jealous as a muthfucka, and they ain't got the heart to come and get what they want the right way. They'd rather see you locked up!"

"True dat, B. True dat!" Stank agreed as he fired up the blunt. "These broke-ass niggas out here today need a bullet in they fuckin' skull!" He continued blowing out a puff of smoke.

"Yeah, I know. That's why I'm thinking 'bout making my move up outta this shit—you know, changing up my shit and going legit. I been talking to Trina bout just packing up and moving outta state, starting over somewhere, getting married and the whole nine."

"Damn, B. You serious 'bout this, huh?" Stank said, blowing smoke out of his lungs.

"As a heart attack, fam! If you want, I can holla at Tee and let him know that you'll be handling the business from now on. I mean, he knows it's all love with you and me. You can have this shit, brah. I'm 'bout to be done! My pops said some shit to me the other day that really put things into perspective for me. He said, 'Beware of wooden nickels.' You know he's always saying some deep shit, but that just stuck with me and made me think about life and what I really want for me and my family, you know? It's like the consequences of this shit has gotten to be too high a price."

"Come on, brah. I know my nigga ain't getting scared on me and shit. We been getting this money far too long for that shaky shit, my nigga." Stank teased.

"Naw. A nigga gotta be thinking out here, brah. I mean you just said it yourself; we been getting this money far too long. When it's all said and done, brah, your life is in your own hands."

"Nigga, now you getting too philosophical on me and shit. It's too early in the morning for this shit. Hell, this ain't but my first blunt. I ain't even got myself together yet, my nigga." Stank laughed, passing the blunt to Danny.

Danny wanted to say more to try to convince Stank it was time to get out of the game, but he knew it was useless. Stank had been through so much in his life. Losing his father at the hands of the police had only fueled his desire to live in defiance of the law, out on the edge. Danny's pops had always told him to never become discombobulated by the revelation of who someone truly is, and he'd discovered who his childhood friend was a long time ago. He knew it would take something more than being tired and leery of the game to convince Stank to get out. He would have to be forced out by other circumstances. Danny just hoped those circumstances wouldn't cost his friend's life or freedom.

CHAPTER 4

STANK DROVE IN silence thinking about his life and all that he'd been through. His father had been killed on his ninth birthday, right in front of him and his little sister, Tanya. They had been coming home from Home-Run-In Pizza parlor celebrating his birthday when they'd been pulled over by the police.

"Here go with this racial profiling shit!" he heard his father say to his mother.

"Just keep your cool, babe. Try not to pist these rednecks off," his mother coached, trying to calm his father down.

"License and registration!" the officer demanded of his father, standing at the driver's door while his partner shone a bright light through the passenger's window where his mom sat.

Disgusted, his father began reaching across his mother's lap to retrieve the credentials from the glove compartment when a thunderous boom rang throughout the car, paralyzing Stank and his sister and causing his mother to release a scream that would forever be etched into his memory bank. The rookie cop on the passenger's side stood there shaking, his revolver trained on Stank's father's lifeless body that lay across his mother's lap.

He'd panicked when Stank's father had reached over to get the demanded documents from the glove compartment.

Stank's mom, Janice, was never the same. She suffered a nervous breakdown that left her emotionally withdrawn from her children and mentally detached from the world around her. Stank and his little sister began calling their aunt Brenda, telling her of their hunger and the lack of food at home. Eventually, she took them in and placed her sister in a nursing home. Brenda had twin boys of her own, Reggie and Renauld, age five at the time, but still she raised Stank and Tanya as if they were her own. Stank's grandmother filed a wrongful death suit against the city of Chicago on behalf of her slain son, but the city was determined to prolong what seemed to be the inevitable for as long as possible.

Stank had grown to hate the police, and his disdain for them left him with little regard for the laws and those attempting to enforce them. His criminal record had consisted of disorderly conduct and assaults on the police and security guards since he was a juvenile.

The conversation he'd just had with Danny played in his mind over and over. He knew Danny was right on point as usual. It was true that niggas were hating, and snitching was at an all-time high. But hell, his paper was nowhere near where Danny's was. He wasn't the type to count another man's money. But he had to keep it real with himself if no one else. And keeping it one hundred, Danny probably had close to a couple million dollars. Stank had been saving, but he had bills because he took care of his entire family. Not saying that Danny didn't have bills or take care of his family; Stank knew he did. Danny just had more than Stank to do it with. Stank had manage to save a few hundred thousand, like maybe about five hundred, but to him that wasn't the kind of money he could retire on and go legit. He needed more and reasoned how he might get it after Danny left the game.

Maybe if I just mess with Tee for a little while longer—say for a few more months—I could stack another quick half mil and chill on out with Joy, he thought, resting his hand on the bottom of the steering wheel. Joy was his girlfriend of five years. He planned to marry her when the time was right. But first he needed to get enough money to leave the streets alone and provide the kind of life she deserved. *I could serve Dee's clientele, plus*

the blocks and my own clients. I could do this in no time. I—His train of
thought was interrupted by the vibrating of his phone.

"Yo what up?" he answered.

"Nephew, this Ray. The Mrs. said you called for me a minute ago."

"Yeah, unc, meet me at the crib, I need you to do something for me.
I'll be there in about twenty minutes." Stank said and hung up. Next, he
called the twins and told them to be around because he would be needing
them to do something in about an hour.

Stank pulled up behind the three-apartment brownstone he shared
with his sister and Aunt Brenda and hopped out the Cutlass to find Ray
waiting on the back steps leading to the basement.

"What up, Unc?" Stank greeted him as he bounced up the walk toward
him. "I see you got your equipment bag and shit ready to take care of
business. That's what I like 'bout you, Unc. You 'bout ya business."

"Nephew, that's all I know is to be about my business. But you the one
on his shit though. That shit dem boys got out there is the bomb! And you
keeps it that way. That's the way to get money. I was sick last night when
I came through and they weren't working!"

"Yeah I know, Unc. But we back on like the Shaw today!"

Once upon a time, Ray had been the man in the hood, sitting on top
of the world. But whatever goes up must come down, and down he had
come never to get back up again. He had the meanest cook game in the
city and was known all over Chicago for his skills. He could blow up one
kilo to almost two with just water. Cats came from all over to employ his
cooking skills. But he especially liked to cook for Stank and Dee because
they paid the best and never wanted him to stretch their cocaine; they
always wanted it cooked the way it was meant to be.

"Hey, babe. How was your day?" Stank asked, greeting Joy with a kiss
as she came through the door of their apartment.

"Too damn long, babe!" she pouted, plopping down onto the couch.
"I thought I was never going to get out of the there. It was meeting after
meeting. My feet are killing me! Please remind me the next time I see
some shoes and say, 'They are just the cutest,' to just stick to comfort." She
frowned, primping her lips.

Stank just smiled and began massaging her feet, relaxing her instantly. It wasn't long before he heard the sounds of her light snore. She was a good woman, Stank thought to himself as he watched her sleeping peacefully. She'd been with him through it all, holding him down even when he didn't have much. It was Joy who brought order to his otherwise chaotic life. Joy worked for Rogers Group Investments as a market analyst. It was through her that Stank was able to clean enough of his money to buy the building they now lived in and fund his sister's college education at Joy's alma mater, Spellman. He knew he should just walk away when Danny did; he and Joy could move away also. They could get married and live a normal life; he felt she deserved that much. He sat there shaking his head, looking at his sleeping angel, and contemplating the possibilities and possible consequences that lay ahead in his future, pending his decision.

CHAPTER 5

"OH NO SHE didn't!" Trina thought out loud as she sized up the woman who'd just cut her in line at Wendy's. "Excuse me, but I know you see me standing here in this line!" Trina said with attitude as she tapped the woman on the shoulder.

"Oh I'm sorry. I don't wanna buy nothing. I was just in the drive-through, and they told me to come inside for my salad. I'm so sorry, girl. I know you probably said, 'This woman done lost her damn mind!'" the woman said, and they both laughed.

"Yeah, I did!" Trina said, and they shared another laugh. "But go on and get that salad, girl, I got time. My lunch break doesn't begin for another fifteen minutes." She winked at the lady.

After lunch, Trina sat at her computer scrolling through the latest Gucci online catalogue, talking to her girlfriend Nee Nee. "Girrrl, have you seen this new shoulder bag Gucci has?" Trina said, almost breathless. "I'm 'bout to order it right now, girl. I gotta have it!" She paused. "Hold on, girl. Let me get my other line; it may be one of the bosses. Thank you for calling Hewlett Packard. This is Trina Brighton speaking. How may I help you today?"

"Hello … Ah is, uh, Samantha Davis in?" Danny said, disguising his voice.

"Hold please!" Trina said, clicking back over to Nee Nee on the other line. "I'ma call you back, girl. This is Daniel on the other line trying to disguise his voice, talking about is Samantha Davis in. This boy gon' make me snap like one of them bitches on the Lifetime channel! He knows I can't stand that trifling slut!" she said, ending the call and clicking back over to Danny.

"This is Samantha speaking!" she said, using the most ghetto tramp voice she could utter.

"Yeah, what's up, baby? We still on foe tonight? You know I can't wait to taste you, girl. Damn, I love it when you sit on my face!" Danny said, trying hard not to laugh, knowing it was still Trina on the phone. You know my woman Trina ain't got nothing on you—with yo fine sexy ass!"

"Nigga you better stop playing before you make me do something to you and that hood rat!" Trina warned.

"Trina? Babe, is this you? How did you get back on the line? I thought I was still talking to my secret lover, Sexy Sam."

"Boy, you got two seconds to cut it out, or I'm cutting you out tonight! Calling me at work with this foolishness, interrupting my busy day," Trina said, trying to sound annoyed.

"Busy doing what? Talking to Nee Nee? Yeah baby. Ya man know you, and I got eyes everywhere on you. See that dude to your left? I got him watching your every move. He types like a thousand words a minute, and he calls me every time you go to the bathroom. Uh-huh, I got eyes all around you, my love," Danny said and they both began laughing.

"Boy, you stuuupid!" she said, still laughing.

"Yeah, that's why you love me, girl," he said, all cocky like.

"I don't even love you. See there. I just love your doggy style!" Trina said, and they broke out laughing again.

If nothing else, Trina and Danny were best friends, and they actually liked the person the other was. Danny and Trina's brother had been friends before he'd been killed in a drive-by shooting. At the time, Trina had been pregnant with her first child by a guy who wanted nothing to do with her or the baby. At her brother's funeral, Danny had consoled both

Trina and her mother, vowing to help raise her unborn child in honor of the friendship he and her brother had shared. The child's father had been gunned down a few months later. Danny never dreamt they'd be engaged to be married just three years later with another baby and one on the way. He'd found true happiness in the most unlikely place—right under his nose.

"Boy, what do you want? You know I can't stand yo butt!" Trina said, smiling into the phone.

"My butt? You can't stand my butt. That's cold, cuz I just love yours. Yeah, I love that fat juicy booty!" Danny said, sounding like Martin Lawrence.

"Boy I'm 'bout to hang up on you in three seconds!"

"OK, it's like this, babe. I need you to do me a favor when you get off work," Danny said, trying to sound helpless.

"What's in it for me?" Trina asked, ready to negotiate for the bag she'd just been eyeing, still on her computer screen in front of her.

"I know you been on that damn computer window-shopping since you got back from lunch. Tell you what. I'll buy you one of the things you saw that you feel you just gotta have," he proposed.

This nigga must have eyes up in here on a bitch for real! she thought to herself, looking around.

"And don't be looking around like that! I told you I got eyes on you my lovely. And I always will!" he said, before giving her the instructions for what he needed done.

"Bitch, I thought you were calling me back earlier!" Nee Nee cut right in when Trina answered the phone.

"Duh! Bitch, I was at work. So, if I didn't call you back, it must have meant I was ahh, let me see … *busy working!*" Trina replied. "And I know Norma Jean taught you how to call someone's house and greet them when they answer," she added.

"Norma Jean ain't taught me a damn thing. And, bitch, you got off work at 4:30. It's now 7:30!" Nee Nee fired back.

"Well, you got me now bitch. What do you want?" Trina said, putting some extra stank on it.

"Thank you, Jesus. Thank you, Lord Jesus. And praise the Lord. Praise the Lord! Sista gurrrl, a bitch almost came through this phone and beat dat ass! Getting all foxy with a pimp. Don't do that shit no mo, Anna Mae!" Nee Nee said making Trina spit up the Pepsi she was drinking through her nose and all over her bed as she burst out laughing.

"Bitch, you are washing my damn comforter! Yo silly ass made me spit up this damn pop, you stupid!" Trina said, still laughing.

"Ride up to the mall with me, girl," Nee Nee pleaded.

"Girl, the mall closes at 9:00, and it's already 7:10," Trina stated.

"I know. But, bitch, I'm already down the street from your house. So, you can just come on out."

Nee Nee had been Trina's best friend since grammar school when some girls from the seventh grade had tried to jump her, and Trina had stepped in to help. They were in the sixth grade. And back then, Trina had a rep for being a fighter, while Nee Nee's was known as being all talk.

"Look, bitch," Trina began as soon as she got in the car. "let's get one motherfucking thing straight. Don't be acting like you got a bitch's card round here, cuz you know I'm too smooth for that hoe! Dropping by my damn house talking 'bout come on out. Bitch, how you know I was gonna say yes? I got a family, bitch. And by the way, *I'm strickly dickly hoe*! You may Need to know, cuz you ain't got a damn thing for me!"

"Another quaalude. She love me again!" Nee Nee said, imitating Al Pacino's character in *Scarface*.

"Bitch, you nutz! You missed your calling; you know that don't you? Because you really did!" Trina said as they both drove off laughing.

"Girl, you know a bitch gotta laugh to keep from crying, all these sad ass excuses for men out here," Nee Nee replied.

"Ut-oh, what done happened now to that baby? Somebody done did her wrong. Tell Mama all about it," Trina said, sounding like she was talking to one of her own children.

"And I'm the crazy one they say, huh?" Nee Nee responded. "Anyway, I'm at home today minding my own business, not fucking with nobody right? OK right, when Mike comes in from the gym all sweaty and looking good and sexy and shit and jumps in the shower. So I'm lying there horny as a mutha wanting some of that good good, tryna be considerate cuz the nigga say he had to hurry to take his mama to the doctor and grocery store. You know the old stanky lady can't get nobody else to let her in their car, cuz it's gonna be smelling like somebody lit a turd up in that bad boy." She fumed.

"Oooh, you know you're wrong for talking about that man's mama," Trina said, holding her hand over her mouth ad trying to suppress a laugh.

"Wrong but true! And, bitch, don't be interrupting me when I'm telling my story! Now listen. So anyway, this nigga's phone is ringing off the hook all while he's in the shower, and I'm thinking this old bitch is bossy right? OK right. You know a bitch like me is nosy, right?"

"Right!" Trina chided in.

"Don't be all quick to jump in now with the rights when a bitch talking 'bout he flaws, when I couldn't get a amen outta ya ass just a minute ago! So anyway, like I was saying, a bitch nosy right? *You betta not say shit!* But I don't even check his shit, you know cuz a bitch playing her part. Instead, I get undressed and slide into the shower with the nigga. Gurrrl, let me tell you, that nigga fucked the shit outta of me like I was the last piece of pussy on God's green earth! I could barely walk when that nigga was through!"

"Wait a minute, bitch you mad cuz yo nigga fucked you good today? See I told you, you were nutz!" Trina said, shaking her head.

"No, dumb dumb, if you let me finish, I'ma tell you what happen. Kay, boo boo? OK, so now we get finished, and he gets dressed and leaves so damn quick that he forget his phone. At first, I didn't even know he'd left it until it starts going off again on the nightstand. I figure I'd answer it and let his mama know that he was on his way—you know, playing my part and shit—when it's some hoe on the phone talking 'bout who is this answering Mike's phone. So I was like, 'Bitch this is his woman. Who is you?' The hoe said she was his wife!"

"Oooh, ouch!" was all Trina could manage to say.

"Yeah, girl. This nigga is married! Over here laying up in my damn bed fucking me and eating my damn food. So I just told the hoe that he'll be there shortly cuz he was done over here and that she didn't have to worry 'bout feeding him cuz he just got finished eating my pussy, so please be a sweetie and wipe his mouth for me cuz I forgot to."

"Has he called you to say anything yet?" Trina inquired.

"Girl, this nigga been blowing my damn phone up! I saw the nigga driving past my house, but my car wasn't there cuz I let my brother use it. But you know what?" Nee Nee said, waving Mike's credit card in the air.

"Bitch you a hot mess. 'Bout to go spend that man's money. He's gonna whup that ass, whup that ass!" Trina teased.

"He's gotta do some catching before he does any whupping—*know that*! Nee Nee laughed as they pulled into the mall's parking lot.

CHAPTER 6

Summer 1997

EVERYTHING WAS GOING smoothly. Troy had been shopping with Tony for a few months. They were copping a kilo, and Tony was fronting them two on the side. Life for them was a lot different now that they were actually seeing some money. They all bought cars and stayed at the mall shopping.

"Aye, bro, I'm 'bout to hit the car wash. Slide up through there and scoop me up. I need to demonstrate with you 'bout something," Phil said, pulling up alongside Bang in front of his mother's house.

Phil sped off, returning his music to the volume that had set off the car alarms on the block when he'd first pulled down the street, gaining the attention of all the chicken heads and old people. Life surely was different now. But all Phil could think of was how much better it could be with Tony's stash. It seemed like every time he'd seen Tony, he looked like he'd just hit the lotto a few times. That big body Benz made him wanna snatch Tony's ass right out of it and put him in the trunk every time he saw him. He felt like Troy was becoming too chummy with Tony. And when the time came to get him, he would be too attached and have reservations about going through with the plan they had made.

"Everything good?" Bang greeted the dudes standing out in front of the car wash as he went around and shook everyone's hand on his way inside.

"Yes, sir, bro. Man, truly everything is good!" They all seemed to chime in unison.

"What's the dealio, bro?" Bang said as he approached Phil, already engaged in a dice game in the back of the car wash.

"You tell me! Bet back, nigga, 10-4," Phil replied, never taking his eyes off the dice game he was in to look at Bang.

The car wash was the neighborhood's recreation center for the hustlers and gamblers. They pitched pennies out front, played pool, and shot dice in the back during business hours. After-hours and on weekends, they fought dogs and had strippers come in. Yeah, this was the neighborhood hangout. They even conducted drugs sales in the bathroom and back office.

Phil had already lost $5,000 and was upset because Jewabee, the cat he was gambling with, was taking his money and talking cash shit all the while. Jewabee was a jet-black Minnesota cat who'd come to Chicago with five of the baddest chicks around and was pimping them. You had to have money to even talk to his whores. They all drove around the city in little CLK Benzes and wore nothing but the latest fashions. Jewabee took the pimp game to another level and had women all over the city wanting to be on his team selling their bodies for him to live like his girls.

"Nigga, I'm 'bout to catch suga diabetes fuckin' wit' you, you so sweet!" Jewabee laughed as the dice rolled to a stop on his point again.

This nigga got a fuckin rabbit's foot or something in his pocket! Phil thought to himself as he yelled, "Bet back, nigga!"

"I'ma let you push that Benz around a couple of blocks for being so damn generous with ya little cop money, my nigga. I'ma even have my best bitch give you some head for free, lil nigga. Shit'd!" Jewabee laughed his famous laugh that made Phil want to duct-tape his ass and take all he had.

"Don't worry, nigga. I got this from ya mama ugly ass! She out on the track now getting a nigga some more," Phil said, now clearly in his feelings.

"Watch ya mouth, lil nigga. And don't get out cha body, cuz I'll put you right back in it!" Jewabee warned with his hand on the pistol in the small of his back.

Phil knew Jewabee had gotten at a few dudes in the past. But to him he was a busta just like every other nigga on the planet was next to him in his mind. He'd secretly been wanting to get at Jewabee since last summer when he had checked him about one of his whores. She was actually digging Phil because of all the noise he and the crew was making, and she liked the way he was so thugged out. Jewabee had pulled up on the corner by the store with her in the car in front of Phil and his guys and started beating her with a hanger, screaming "Tell dat nigga to come save yo ass!" Phil had taken it as disrespect, cuz while he wanted to push the nigga's shit back right then and there, he didn't want to be seen as a captain save-a-hoe. His motto was real niggas don't save whores. So to be put on the spot like that was embarrassing. He told the crew that, if Jewabee ever jumped out there again, he was gonna put some hot shit off in him.

Phil left the dice game $7,000 down with a chip on his shoulder as they jumped in Bang's SS Impala.

"Ride down on that nigga Troy, right quick," he instructed as they pulled off from the wash. "We need to do this shit with that nigga Tony ASAP. He's ripe for the pickin!" he said, reaching for the blunt in Bang's ashtray.

"I don't know why we ain't grabbed that nigga yet," Bang said, turning down Troy's baby mother's block.

"I told the nigga to get the chump relaxed and shit, you know, used to fucking with us. But this nigga acting like he falling in love with 'im, like they fucking or something," Phil said, hitting the blunt.

This nigga Phil on some ole jealousy type shit with all that. I ain't on that shit, Bang thought to himself. *I just want the money.*

They pulled in front of Renee's house. It was true that the plan was to get Tony to let his guard down and reveal where he had some dope and money stashed, and Troy has already found where the shit was. What confused Bang was why they hadn't just taken the easy lick and gotten the fuck on. It seemed that Troy was trying to make some kind of bond with him, and Phil really wanted to be the one close to him. But since he couldn't, he wanted to do something to him instead of just robbing the house.

"What's the demo?" Troy said, hopping in the back seat.

"What's up with ya boy?" Phil cut to the chase.

Troy filled them in on all the details of Tony's daily routine and the lay out of his house in the city out south. "But like I told you, we could just hit the crib while the nigga's out and about in the streets taking care of business," Troy finished. He didn't see Tony as the type of dude they had to rob to get on. Tony was the type of cat who wanted to see you doing good. He was generous with that shit and was feeding a lot of niggas in the city. He wasn't nothing like the normal niggas they were trying to catch with their pants down, so to speak.

"Nigga you can go ahead on with that soft shit. We grabbing that nigga like we planned, and his people betta run that money. Or your little BFF ain't gonna make it!" Phil said with finality in his voice.

"Nigga, it's whatever! And only bitches got BFFs. A nigga ain't got a soft bone in his body!" Troy said, trying to save face.

"Good, cuz you need to be on top of this shit the way Renee taking all ya muthafuckin dough!" Phil said, laughing as he dumped the tobacco from the blunt into an empty Big Gulp cup preparing to roll up.

Bang joined in the laughter.

"Renee gots my shorty, nigga," Troy retorted, narrowing his eyes at Bang. "And I knooow *you* ain't up there laughing, nigga, the way Pretty gots yo ass opened the fuck up chasing her all around the town buying her shit to wear for the other niggas she round here fuckin'! Vicky Secrets and shit! Nigga, I know you ain't laughing, ole coo ass nigga!"

"Later foe all that shit, niggas. Right now the business at hand is getting that nigga!" Phil cut in, and they began mapping out the plan to grab Tony.

CHAPTER 7

TONY EXITED THE Dan Ryan Expressway at 76th Street and pulled into the Walgreen's parking lot. Just as he put the car in park, the rain began cascading down as if on cue. "Fuck!" he thought aloud as he shut the car off and reached in the back seat for the newspaper he'd bought earlier that morning. Today had been fucked from the moment he'd woken up and had to piss.

"Ahh shit!" was all he could manage to say, trying to endure the pain racing through his dick that felt like rusty razor blades being pulled through by a powerful magnet. He wanted to kill that fucking bitch and Jewabee for this shit. *Top notch my ass!* he thought as he got dressed and went to the clinic to get the shot he was so accustomed to that they knew him by name and face.

"Not again, Mr. Hernandez?" Dr. Myles said as she entered the examination room. "You know condoms will prevent this and quite possibly keep you from contracting something more serious like HIV or AIDS."

It was all the same speech to Tony. He knew he was taking chances by not using protection, but he didn't like rubbers and refused to use them. "Do you use condoms, doc?" he asked in broken English.

29

"I'm married, Mr. Hernandez. So no I do not use condoms. But if I weren't, I would definitely use protection during intercourse. The question is, Why don't you feel protection is important?" she countered.

"Well it's like this, doc, to be honest. It don't feel as good with a rubber on as it does without one. I know how it sounds, but it's true," he explained.

"Well did you know that there are products on the market that increase stimulation for those who use condoms and even extra-sensitive condoms?" she informed him.

"I guess I didn't know that, doc," he responded, studying her perfect figure as she filled out the prescription he'd need to cure his current condition.

Tony had a shitload of things to do today. He had a shipment coming in. The cable at the house out south had gone out in last night's storm, and the cable company had said someone should be home between 12:00 p.m. and 4:00 p.m. Not to mention the last shipment had been sieged by the coast guard down in Miami, and his brother-in-law was pitching a bitch about that like he was to blame. Damn it, he hated him! Plus, he still had to count all this damn money and get it packed up to be shipped to Colombia.

He'd driven to the house on the South Side and waited for the cable company, hoping he hadn't already missed them. He couldn't—under any circumstances—live without cable for one second. The NBA was truly fantastic! He wouldn't miss a single game for the world! Finally done with all that he had to do for the day, he headed out to get the prescription that he'd already dropped off earlier filled.

Hopping out of the car, Tony jogged to the store's entrance holding the newspaper over his head and attempting to stay as dry as possible. He noticed a homeless guy standing under the shelter of the building's structure.

"Can you spare some change?" asked the homeless man as Tony passed by going into the store.

"See me when I come out, bro," he replied, walking through the automatic doors that swung open as he passed the sensor. Tony grabbed the prescription and was out in no time.

True to his word, he handed the homeless man a ten-dollar bill on his way back to the car. He made a dash out into the rain, catching the end of what sounded like, "Thank you, Jesus!" coming from the homeless guy.

Then, out of nowhere, two masked figures came up on both sides of him with guns drawn.

"Oh *shit*!" Tony said as his heart rate sped up.

"Not here, asshole!" one of the masked men said as they forced him to the rear of the car and made him open the trunk and get inside.

"You won't be needing this!" said the other masked figure, taking his cell phone.

"At least not for now you won't." This came from other man as he slammed the trunk shut.

Tony was scared shitless as he felt the car come to a complete stop and the engine shut off. When the trunk was popped open, he realized he was inside his garage on Loomis Avenue. "If it's money you want, that ain't no problem. You ain't gotta kill me. I can show you where the money is," he said, terrified as they snatched him out the trunk and onto his feet.

"Oh we know you got the money. And yes you are gonna show us where it's at. What I don't know is if I'ma let you live or not!" said the masked dude who was clearly in charge.

Tony took them through the house to the front door. *Thwack*! one of the robbers hit him upside the head with his gun.

"You think this some kind of game, muthafucka?"

"Naw man, the sta-sta-stash is under the front door's threshold. I-I-I wouldn't play no games, I swear!" said Tony nervously. "You j-j-just gotta flip the third switch on the wall over there," Tony explained, pissing the fucking razor blades again.

The masked man in charge waved his gun, giving Tony permission to go and flip the switch to retrieve the money.

"I-I-I just gotta open the door now, and the money is there," Tony said after flipping the switch. The leader waved his gun again, giving the OK, and Tony opened the front door and the threshold raised. He began pulling money from the space below tossing it over toward the feet of the robber closest to him. The other masked man kicked him onto his side out of the way and began retrieving the cash himself.

He couldn't believe all the money he felt in the floor. Excitedly, he threw stack after stack out at his partner's feet. His partner kept his gun trained on Tony, where he lay on his side just a few feet away.

The scenario seemed to go on for ages. Tony felt like twenty hours had passed. His mind raced with fear that they would, in fact, kill him after they'd gotten what they had come for. His only chance at surviving would be getting to the gun he kept strapped under the coffee table just to his left. He saw the masked man with the gun on him looking from him to his partner and the money he continued pulling from the floor; and knew he had to time it just right to have even a remote shot at making it out alive.

Now! he thought as he stretched out, reaching for the firearm. No sooner than his hand touched it he was firing. *Boom, boom, boom* went the first shots from Tony's gun. A bullet struck the robber who was digging out the money once in the ass, causing him to scream out in pain and his partner to return fire. Tony shot two more times before making a run for it to the kitchen, heading for the garage where they'd come in. Just as he made it to the entrance of the garage door, a third masked figure stepped out and shot him point-blank in the face, ending his attempted escape.

Bang lay across the back seat moaning in pain from the bullet wound in his left buttocks.

"We gone drop you off at the hospital and then shoot to the tip and put away the money and these burners. You should be done by then," one of the two said from the front seat.

Bang couldn't be sure who'd said it but disagreed, still moaning in pain. "No the fuck y'all not fitting to drop me off at no fuckin' hospital and bounce!"

"Nigga, we ain't about to be up in no damn hospital with these muthafuckin burners and yo ass laying up there with a bullet in ya ass! Fuck is you thinking, nigga?" Phil began. "Shit, and quit acting like a little bitch, nigga. Man the fuck up! It ain't nothing but a fuckin flesh wound, nigga, in and out."

"Fuck you, nigga! When did you become a doctor? You don't know what the fuck kinda wound this is," Bang returned between moans.

"Quit all that muthafuckin moaning back there, nigga. You sound like a little bitch getting fucked!" Troy spat, not looking back.

"Nigga, you betta be figuring out what the fuck you gone tell Five-O, cuz they gone be askin' all sorts of questions when they show up," he added.

"Look, bro, tell them you was on the pay phone and somebody drove by and shot outta the window and kept going," Phil instructed. "Here pull over in front and let this nigga out. He can hop around to the emergency entrance," he told Troy.

"Nigga, fuck that. Nigga, take me to the muthafuckin doe. I ain't hoppin' around nowhere!" Bang retorted.

"They gots cameras at the entranceway, dumb ass nigga. You tryna get us popped or something? Just get the fuck outta the damn car. Shit you wasting time, nigga!" Phil said through clenched teeth.

———⊱✦⊰———

"What's your emergency, sir?" asked the tired nurse behind the desk as Bang hopped forward.

"I been shot!" He moaned in pain. "Somebody rode by and shot me when I was standing at the pay phone."

Without delay, he was taken to a room closed in by curtains and laid on a bed. Two detectives came in to interview him in less than fifteen minutes to see if he knew who had shot him and would be willing to press charges.

"I don't know who the hell shot me. They rode by when I was on the pay phone with my back turned!"

"How do you know it was a 'they' and not a 'him' or 'her' if your back was turned?" asked one of the two.

"Look, man, I don't know if it was a him, a them, or a it! I just know that I'm shot!"

Seems like it's always the same with the cops. They interrogate the victims like it's all their fault, while the real criminals get away, one of the nurses thought to herself. *Good thing for this poor guy it's just a flesh wound, in and out.* She said to herself after all she'd seen on the job, as she stitched his wound.

Later, Bang limped out of the hospital with crutches under one arm and Pretty under the other.

"How did you get up here?" he inquired as they exited the emergency room doors.

"Phil came by my house and told me you needed me to come get you from here, and he gave me his car. He said to bring you to the Courtyard Marriott. Said you had a room up there and to give you this key card," she explained, stuffing the card into his pocket.

Meanwhile, he just kinda looked stuck; he was taking in what she was saying and thinking of his cut of the money all at once.

"What the hell happened to you, boy? Are you into it with somebody, babe?"

"Look, I told you 'bout asking me about my business. I ain't into it with no damn body. A muthafucka rode by and shot outta the damn window!"

Shot outta the damn window my ass, nicca! Pretty thought to herself. *This nicca must think I'm stupid as he is. Done tried to rob the wrong muthafaya this time, and they shot the shit outta his ole stupid ass.* She drove on in silence.

CHAPTER 8

DANNY AND STANK pulled up to the club and observed the people waiting in line to get in. They sat double parked checking out the women who'd come out in flocks to party tonight.

"Dayum! Look at the ass on lil mama over there!" Stank said, passing Danny the blunt.

"Aww dayum nigga, look at that face! That's gotta be a dude dawg. That's a nigga, brah. You trippin'," Danny said, cracking up.

"Naw, nigga, you trippin'. With a ass like that, shorty can get it tonight," Stank said sipping his Rémy Martin VSOP.

They sat and smoked another blunt while they finished their drinks, hollering at different women they saw on their way into the club. They knew so many women from hanging out in the clubs and around the city that there were very few who they didn't already know and had their way with. That was the thing about getting money in a city like Chicago; the more money you got, the more pussy you commanded.

"Hey, Dee, what's up? I see you and Stank sitting out here watching bitches like y'all some kind of talent scouts or something," Pretty said as she and her girl Tricey approached Danny's Range Rover.

"What kind of talents do you got, ma?" Danny asked, hugging her out the window and palming her ass, giving it a nice squeeze.

"The kind that'll make a nicca leave home! Now quit it before somebody sees you with your damn hands all on my ass and shit, boy," Pretty said pulling from his embrace.

"Ain't no boys up in here! What y'all getting into tonight, Ms. Pretty?" Danny asked, leaning back into his already reclined seat.

"We gone see if we can get up in this damn club. Shit, the line is all the way to the corner," she said.

"If I get y'all in pass all that, y'all gotta be rollin' with us tonight when this shit's over. I mean at least to breakfast or something," Danny proposed, smiling.

"I don't know. I heard 'bout y'all, Dee. Y'all might be too much for me and my girl," Pretty said seductively, before giggling.

"Come on, hop in. We gone finish this blunt and the rest of this drink befoe we go in," Danny instructed, popping the door locks.

The club was packed when they entered. Busta's new joint was blasting through the speakers, and everybody was putting their hands where his eyes could see.

"Hey, Dee!" A waitress approached, giving Danny a hug as they made their way to VIP.

"What's good, Kim? Aye, bring a couple bottles of Crystal up to VIP and some Belvy." Danny spoke into her ear before releasing his embrace.

"What you drinking, Big Stank?" Kim asked, giving him a hug to show love and squeezing his ass.

"The usual, Rémy VSOP straight up!" they both said, as if reading from a script.

By the end of the night, Pretty and Tricey were drunk and horny as hell. Stank drove while Danny sat in the back with Pretty's head in his lap.

"Dayum, she ain't playing no games!" Stank thought out loud, looking through the rearview at Pretty's head bobbing up and down like an oil drill digging for oil as he drove.

Danny didn't respond. All he could do was hold the back of her head and enjoy her soft, warm mouth as she attempted to take him all in and swallow him whole. Tricey was on Stank as he pulled into the parking garage of Danny's building, massaging his member through his pants aggressively.

"I can't wait until we can start our fun. I got a real treat for you!" she said, hot enough to melt rubber.

"Have a good night, Mr. Robertson," the night guard at the desk said to Danny as they passed by on their way to the elevators.

"Buenos noches, Carlos. I surely intend to," Danny replied.

The next morning, Stank dropped Pretty and Tricey back off at Tricey's car near the club where they'd left it the night before. Returning to Danny's apartment, Stank found Danny in a trancelike state starring at the TV.

"Fuck wrong with you, brah? That bitch put some kind of spell on you last night or something?" Stank joked.

Danny just sat there looking at the TV and shaking his head before saying, "You ain't gonna believe this."

Stank came around and looked at the screen. "Ain't that Tee's crib over on Loomis?" was all he could say before he realized what he was hearing the reporter saying.

"Breaking news," the reporter was saying. "I repeat, home invasion and possible homicide here at 9237 South Loomis. Neighbors say they heard gunshots around 10:30 last night and called the police. Here's one of the residents who says he heard the shots."

The camera panned to the neighbor, who was all worked up. "Yeah I heard the shots somewhere around 10:25 last night. Me and my son was about to walk the dog when I heard *boom, boom, boom*! Then it was like World War III broke out up in there. It was just bad. I mean really bad! I used to see the guy that lived there. He'd come and go and was polite enough for the most part. Always spoke to everybody. I can't say what he was into, but it had to be something cuz he drove really nice cars. And the lady that lives next door to him said she heard voices talking about money."

"I'm Denise Hill for Fox 32 News. Back to you, Tom."

Danny had been telling Tony to stop using them hood cribs to hold his stash and doing business out of them for the longest. He'd been trying to convince him to get an apartment in the building he lived in or one like it with security. Tony wouldn't listen, though, because he owned so many houses scattered about the city's South Side. He couldn't see any reason not to use them the way he did.

———————

Danny made his way to Northwestern Hospital where Tony had been taken. It was a madhouse of police and reporters.

"Tony Hernandez's room please," Danny said as he approached the nurses' station.

"And you are?" said the over worked nurse.

"His brother. How is he doing, ma'am?" Danny replied.

"I can't discuss his condition. You'll have to speak with his doctor. I'll page the doctor for you. Please have a seat in the waiting area."

A short while later, a tiny Asian woman appeared. "Mr. Hernandez?" she called out, and Danny stood to see the little woman in blue scrubs approaching his direction.

"Hi, Mr. Hernandez. I'm Dr. Choo. I operated on your brother last night when he was brought in."

"How's he doing, doc?" Danny asked.

"Well brain surgery is very complex to begin with. Your brother was shot at point-blank range, which probably saved his life—that and the quick response of the neighbors. The bullet entered just above his left eye and pierced his frontal lobe before exiting at the top of his skull. He's in a medically induced coma right now. And it's too early to know if we're out of the woods just yet. We'll be monitoring him closely over the next forty-eight hours."

"Pierced his frontal lobe? What does that mean, doc? And how serious is it?" Danny questioned.

"The frontal lobe is one of four lobes located in the brain's cerebral cortex that regulates different functions. The frontal lobe regulates movement and cognitive activities like planning, deciding, and pursuing goals. Biological functions for personality and temperament reside there as well."

"So what are you saying, doc? He won't be able to move or think again?" Danny pressed.

"Again, Mr. Hernandez, it's too early to know if any of these functions will be affected by his injuries. But you can go in and see him just for a few minutes," Dr. Choo said before stepping away.

<hr>

Tony lay in ICU at Northwestern Hospital on Chicago's North Side. He'd been airlifted there the night of the robbery three weeks ago and remained in a coma. His mother and sister Elise had flown in from Colombia and kept vigil at his bedside. Everything was touch-and-go at the moment. The doctors were meeting at 2:00 p.m. that afternoon to decide their next course of action. The bullet had exited Tony's skull, but the damage done to his frontal lobe was the focus of concern for them at the present, and due to swelling, it was still too soon to assess.

"Hey, Elise. Hi, Ms. Hernandez, have the doctors said anything yet? Has anything changed with his condition?" Danny asked as he gave both Tony's sister and mother comforting hugs and a kiss on the cheek.

"Who would do such a thing to my Antonio, Danny?" Ms. Hernandez asked with tears streaming down her face.

"I don't know, Ms. Hernandez. But I'm gonna find out."

"And I want to know the minute you do!" Elise cut in with fire in eyes that refused to be smoldered by her building tears.

Danny looked over at the silk robe and slippers he'd brought on his second visit to see his fallen comrade and put his face down into his hands. It all seemed unreal to him, like a bad dream that he couldn't awake from. Tony was more than just a connect to him; he was a brother. Danny exited the room before the tears filling his eyes began falling.

Elise followed him out hot on his heels. "Let me talk to you for a minute, Dee," she said, stopping as the door closed behind her, giving him time to compose himself. "The detectives found blood at Tony's house that wasn't his, and they think it may belong to one of his assailants. They also found his car abandoned out west near Maywood. There were prints everywhere—in both the house and car. They may contact you if any of the prints are yours."

"Tee didn't have too many people at that house. I don't know about the car, though, because he was always out and about. And you know he's a man of the people. I stayed on him about them damn houses he owns in the hood. I told him time and again to get an apartment in one of the buildings I live in downtown, where not just anyone can walk in without being checked in at the front desk. And if anything looks suspicious, they wouldn't hesitate to call the police. I would sometimes see him, and he'd have some new cat with him like they were best buddies. But I wouldn't even try to meet them. *Damnit!*" Danny frowned, no longer able to hold back the tears.

They embraced one another and cried on each other's shoulder.

"I want the name of the person or people responsible for this, Dee. Anybody you can think of who you remember seeing with Tony, I wanna know their names and what they look like. Will you do that for me, Dee?" Elise pleaded with tears still running down her cheeks.

CHAPTER 9

Late summer, 1997

"CHECKMATE!" MUSTAFA SAID concerning Ock's king

"Yeah I slept on that move right there. I forgot all about that bishop over in the corner lampin' like a sniper," Ock said, conceding to the loss.

"Gotta make a call, beloved. We'll pick up after chow later on. As-salamu alaykum," Mustafa said, getting up from the table.

"Wa alaykumu salam," Ock responded.

"This is a prepaid call from an inmate at a federal correctional institution. You will not be charged for this call. This call is from ... *Daniel Robertson*. To accept, press five."

"What's up, Pops?" Danny said as soon as the call was connected.

"What's up with you, young buck? How's your mother and my grandbabies? And you betta be treatin' my daughter-in-law right!"

"Everybody's good on this end, Pops. How are things going on yours?" Danny replied.

"Things are lookin' good on the appeal. I spoke with the lawyer today, and he says he has the brief done. Says he's gonna send it to me to check it out before he files it," Mustafa informed him.

"Yeah, I took him the money yesterday. Did he tell you?" Danny asked.

"He said you came by the office and that y'all spoke for a minute. Inshallah I'll be home before long. Patience is a virtue and the key to moderation, you know," Mustafa said. He had been locked up for the past twenty years in federal prison, serving a life sentence for drugs. "When you bringing my grandkids this way, son?"

"We coming next weekend, Pop. Did you get the money I sent this morning?"

"I haven't checked my account today, son. But if you sent it, I'm sure it's there. How's Trina? I really hope you doing right by that girl, son. She's a good girl for you."

"I got this, Pops. I got this!" Danny responded, confident and cocky.

"You may not be in the mood to learn what you think you already know I guess," Mustafa said, quoting lyrics from one of the Isley Brothers' old songs. That was his way, always using the simplest of things to make the strongest points.

"Remember this, son. Love seeks to satisfy others at the expense of self, while lust seeks to satisfy self at the expense of others." This time, he was quoting Pastor Benard, a Christian preacher that his cellmate often listened to.

"A'ight, Pops, I feel you. We gonna see you next weekend. Let me get off this phone before these police I just passed pull me over," he said, ending the call.

"Main line!" the correctional officer yelled, standing in the entranceway of the cell house as he released the unit for lunch.

"You going to chow, Aki?" Ock asked Mustafa as he came out of the laundry room.

"Yeah, I'ma go over and get my common fare and bring it back,"

Mustafa replied, referring to the special religious meal he received each day per his Islamic beliefs.

⊷∘⊶

"Daniel Robertson, report to the visiting room. You have visitors."

Hearing the visiting room's officer announcement over the loudspeaker, Mustafa dressed for his visit. As he thought of what it would feel like to spend time with his grandchildren without the restraints of prison, a smile crossed his face.

"Have a good one!" one of the guys on the unit with him yelled as he made his way out the door of the housing unit.

It's always a good one when your loved ones come to see you, he thought as he continued down the walkway toward the visiting room.

"Granddaddy! *Granddaddy!*" Lil Jay screamed as he raced to Mustafa's arms, with his little sister Heaven close behind.

Mustafa lived for this moment; his grandbabies were his world. His cell was filled with pictures of them and the pictures they'd made in school and summer camp for him.

"How's Granddaddy's babies doing?" he said, scooping them up into his arms and carrying them to where their parents were seated.

"Hey, Dad!" Trina said as Mustafa bent to hug her where she sat holding the newest addition to their clan, little Danny, who they called Junior.

"Wow, is that my little man? Look how big he is! How many months is he now?"

"Six," Trina said, smiling as she passed Junior to his grandfather's waiting arms.

Mustafa sat holding his grandson for the first time with tears in his eyes. "He looks just like you did, son. And look at him checking me out!"

"Yeah, Dad. He doesn't do much crying either; he's a good baby," Trina said with pride.

"You keeping this dude in check?" he said, nodding in Danny's direction with a smile and wink.

"I see you're still hitting the gym, Pops. That's good, cuz yo grandkids don't want no fat old man for a granddaddy when you get out of this place," Danny said changing the subject and giving his father a slap on the back.

"Wish I could say the same for you, son. Looks like you picking up weight, boy! What are you feeding my son, girl? You betta get him to the gym before these babies have a fat daddy," he said, laughing.

"I know Pops. She's tryna get me all fat making all that good food and then leavin' it in the microwave for me when I come home at night," Danny joked.

"Well, if he'd come home at dinner time and eat with his family like normal people do, he'd burn off all those calories by bedtime!" Trina responded in a matter-of-fact tone, shaking her head.

"She just don't want no other woman to want me Pops, don't listen to none of that crap!" he retorted jokingly.

"Boy, don't nobody want your butt but me. Keep on, and I'm not gonna want you!" Trina warned, giving his arm a playful pinch.

"That's right, baby. Keep this knucklehead in check out there!" Mustafa said, laughing at the two of them.

"I try, Dad. But you know he thinks he's slick. And I don't wanna end up in here for doing something to him and one of his little girlfriends," she said with a sigh, like she just didn't know what to do with Danny and had given up.

Danny just played like he wasn't paying attention to her comment about his little girlfriends as he opened the snacks the kids had bought from the vending machine. "And I know he hears me," Trina said, slapping Danny upside the head. "Ole bigheaded butt!"

"So how was the drive down?" Mustafa asked changing the subject.

"It was pretty quiet out there, Pops. Don't see too many cars out on the road this time of morning, so we made good timing," Danny said.

"Yeah, Dad. We got here around 7:00 this morning but stopped so the kids could eat and ended up getting here at like 9:15 after they'd stopped letting people in," Trina chimed in.

"Yeah, they stop processing visitors around that time because they're about to do the institutional count. They don't start letting visitors in again until it clears," Mustafa explained while giving Heaven a pony ride on his knee. He loved her little giggles and beautiful smile.

"So, how's the case coming along, Dad? Have you received the brief yet?" Trina asked, stealing one of Lil Jay's cookies as he studied his grandfather's giant hands.

"I'm working on some things with the lawyer. I got the brief and read it a few days ago, but I want him to change a couple of things, so it won't get filed until next week—if we file it then. I think we may wait to see how the Supreme Court rules on a case before them now, that resembles my own. If they rule in the guy's favor, the same will apply for me too, and I'll be home soon after that."

"Do you need to use the restroom, Heaven baby?" Trina asked her daughter because she was dancing in place.

"Nooo!" said little Heaven. She shook her head, and the barrettes in hair slapped together, making a *click-clack* sound.

"Then why are you dancing in place? Come on, we're gonna go try anyway just to be sure. And you too!" she said to Lil Jay, standing to take their little hands.

"I heard what happened to Tony, son? How's he doing? And how are you holding up?" asked a concerned Mustafa when Trina and the kids were out of earshot.

"He's coming around. Just woke up out his coma a few days ago. Doctors say he's a lucky man."

"No such thing as luck, son. Allah is merciful! How about you though, son? How are you really doing?"

"I'm good, Pops. It's just that, when something like this hit so close to home, it makes you think more deeply about life and what's important to you. You know?"

"Yeah, I understand that son. And I'm glad you think like that. Come on, let's take a walk outside on the patio. I wanna talk to you about something," Mustafa suggested.

They sat in the far end corner of the patio connected to the visiting room, where they could talk in private.

"Do you know some cat out there called Bang?" Mustafa asked.

"Naw, but I think I may have heard the name before. I'm sure it's nobody I know though."

"Well, word in here is he's the dude behind what happened to Tony.

45

These lil cats in here talk just like women, son. They talk so much about other people's business, it doesn't even make sense. I guess they're supposed to be friends with him or something. I don't know. But they talkin about all the money he supposed to have now. You gotta watch out for cats like that, son. You have a wonderful family, and these rivers are grimy. They'll try to get you where it hurts to get at what you got if they want it," Mustafa said.

"I feel you, Pops. I don't do the flashy thing no more, wearing all the jewelry and whatnot." He knew he was ready to reveal his plans, and he met his dad's gaze. "To be honest, Pops, I'm trying to make my way outta this right now. It's not just cuz of what happened to Tee. I was already on my way out. This just confirmed that it was the right thing to do. I'm just wrappin' up a few lose ends, and I'm out."

CHAPTER 10

DANNY DROVE IN silence, totally engulfed in thoughts about what his father had told him. He knew he'd heard the name Bang in the streets before. He was certain he'd heard Pretty mention the name to her girlfriend Tricey the night he and Stank had them at his apartment. He wished he could call Stank right that moment, but Trina was in the truck with him. *Damn!* he thought, gripping the steering wheel tightly.

"What's wrong, babe? Is everything OK?" Trina asked, rubbing his arm that rested on the console between them. "You haven't said two words since we left the prison."

"Everything's fine, babe. Just thinking 'bout Pops; that's all. I've been coming to see him in prison all my life, havin' to leave him behind when it's time to go. It still messes with my head sometimes. I just hope this time he comes home for real you know?" Danny said, camouflaging his true thoughts with deeper feelings about his father.

"Bae, I worry about you every time you walk out that door. All while I'm at work and even when we're at home together, still I worry. What would we do if something were to happen to you?" Tina said as she continued rubbing his arm.

"Nothing's gonna happen to me, babe. I told you that I'm leaving this alone, and for you to pick a city anywhere in the world you wanna live, and we're gonna move there. Right now, I'm just tyin' up some loose ends, and then I'm out—two weeks tops! I bet you ain't even been on top of your business with finding a place you wanna live, have you?" Danny said, interlocking his fingers with hers.

"What you want for dinner tonight, bae?" Trina asked.

"Naw, don't be tryna change the subject with yo slick ass, girl," Danny said, smiling at the thought of her evading his question.

"I'm on top of it. Just haven't made up my mind yet. But I promise I'm gonna make it up soon. I promise. Now what do you want to eat tonight, boy?"

"You!" Danny said, licking his lips.

"That's dessert," Trina replied seductively.

"I gotta make a quick run, babe. Just surprise me. Anything is cool as long as I get you for dessert!"

"Well, you'd better not take too long cuz your dessert is already hot enough to melt!" she teased, crossing her legs tightly and rubbing them against each other.

Danny and Stank rode for a few blocks in the neighborhood while he told Stank what his father had revealed to him about the robbery.

"I know that nigga Bang, he be out east around 75th and Kingston in that area. I know him from out in Glenwood at the skating rink. He used to be with this nigga I went to school with," Stank said, pulling up a mental picture.

"Small fucking world," Danny said, hitting the blunt. "I think I heard that bitch Pretty talkin' bout that nigga the other night at the apartment."

"Way ahead of you, fam. We gotta get them hoes to open up and tell us what we need to know," Stank said, rubbing his hands together, smiling.

"Yeah, see what them hoes up to this weekend. Maybe we'll shoot out to Vegas and take 'em along—see what they talkin 'bout," Danny instructed before dropping Stank back at his car.

When Danny made it home, all the lights were out except for the glow of the flat screen in his and Trina's bedroom. It had to have been three hours since he'd dropped her and the kids off and gone to meet Stank. He followed the glow to their bedroom, where he found Trina fast asleep.

After undressing down to his boxer briefs, he pulled back the covers to get into bed with his angel. And there she was—T-shirt and no panties. The sight of her neatly shaped pubic hairs was like a magnet commanding his dick to stand at attention immediately. Danny quickly slipped out of his underwear and into bed behind her. He kissed her on the neck beneath her earlobe, her favorite spot.

Trina stirred as he continued kissing her from behind. His kisses trailed her neckline to her shoulders to her back as he caressed her right breast, massaging it gently and causing her to moan as her juices began to flow. Danny kissed her on her lower back and ran his tongue between the length of her perfectly shaped ass before turning her over and continuing his journey south to her wonderland. Beginning with a kiss as soft as a feather's touch, he greeted the guardians at the gate to her beautiful burning inferno.

"Oooh!" Trina moaned at the connection, causing him to probe further with another of the holy kisses he'd placed on her lower lips. He licked her clit, provoking the slightest tremble of an oncoming spasm. He licked her again, receiving the same reaction before blowing a gentle breeze on it, causing it to pulsate and swell. He took it between his lips and tongue delicately, licking and sucking it with a passionate gentle force.

She clutched his head at his ears from both sides in an attempt to endure the unnerving ride to ecstasy as he launched his lips and tongue curiously at her matrix over and over. "Oh, Dee, babe!" Trina cried helplessly as her back arched, and she released the sweet juices of her nectar he'd been scavenging for.

"Put it in, babe. You gotta put it in!" Trina moaned, unable to ignore the burning desire building to feel him deep inside her love canal. With her legs still resting on his shoulders, he entered her again with long strokes. "Oh I'm coming, babe," she whined, grasping at the sheets as if they could help her hang on to her sanity.

Danny increased the pace of his strokes as she met each one with thrusting rebuttals of her own. "Who's pussy is this? Who's pussy is this?"

he grunted breathlessly, laboring to bring her to the threshold of paradise yet again.

"This yo pussy, babe. It's all yours," she whined. "Oh, I'm coming again. Babe, come wit' me!" Trina cried in a weakened whimper.

They collapsed into each other's arms as they climaxed, breathing at a runner's pace. Danny lay with Trina in his arms, her head resting on his chest, and thinking of her and the children. They were his world, and he couldn't bear to think of life without them.

"What's on that beautiful mind of yours, babe?" she asked, looking up into his eyes.

"You, babe—you and our beautiful children. I don't know how I got to be so lucky to have you all," he replied, tightening his embrace.

"We're the lucky ones, babe. Not many men would or even could be the man you are to us! You're my everything I need and want in a man." She lifted her lips to meet his for a brief kiss.

They held each other for a while longer in silence, cloaked by the darkness of their bedroom.

"Can we sleep with it in tonight, babe?" She wanted to sleep with Danny's member inside her as they did so many nights after making love.

CHAPTER 11

Spring 1998

IT HAD BEEN about a year since the robbery. Bang had settled into the new life that money had created for him. He cherished his black Escalade almost as much as he did Pretty. She, on the other hand, cherished the shopping sprees he was now able to provide more than anything. He had taken her shopping everywhere—from the Magnificent Mile downtown to the shopping district in New York, and she had the wardrobe to prove it. Bang started spending all his time with her, going to the movies, out to dinner, to carnivals, and of course to the mall to shop. He even began taking her out stepping. He no longer hung out in the hood except to pick up money or drop off the drugs to his workers on the blocks they were hustling on. He and Pretty rented an apartment in Crestwood, a suburb not too far from the city, where he stayed most of the time when he wasn't making his rounds or out with Pretty.

Bang left the car wash, heading through the old neighborhood to check on his guys before he headed back out to Crestwood, where Pretty was waiting to go to the movies and out to dinner.

"What's up, bro?" He greeted Troy as he pulled alongside Troy's Aurora double parked in the street, blocking another car in its parking space.

"What's crack-a-lackin' bro; man?" Troy replied.

"Shit, me and wifey 'bout to hit the show downtown at the Water Tower. I was sliding through to get my whip washed and check on Ski and Zoe n'em. What you 'bout to get into?" he asked as another car behind him blew its horn, wanting to pass them.

"Aye, bro, pull over for a second. I need to holler at cha for a minute," Troy said as he turned back to the female he had blocked in her parking spot, preventing her departure. "So what's up? You gonna hit a nigga up or what?" he pressed as he leaned over toward his passenger's window.

"Damn, bro; man, you gone make me get one of these muthafuckas. This nice as hell!" Troy said as he slid into the passenger side of Bang's truck.

"What's the biz, bro. Everything good?" Bang asked as they shook hands.

"Here draw off this, bro," Troy said, pulling out a sandwich bag of marijuana. "I got twenty pounds of this the other day from my Arab buddy up at the phone shop."

"This the shit right here, nigga! What you letting it go for?" Bang said excitedly as he smelled the contents of the bag, checking out its texture.

"I ain't movin it like that. This goin' in sacks. But I'll let you get one of 'em for $2,500 cuz it's you, bro."

Bang quickly counted out the money and handed it over to Troy without delay.

"Pull around the corner to Renee's crib. I got a couple of them over there she 'bout to sack up for the block," he instructed.

<hr />

"Boy, where you at? You know the movie starts at 9:15, and it's already 7:30!" Pretty barked into the phone as soon as Bang answered.

"I'm on my way now, Ma. main thing is don't panic," Bang said, ever so smooth as he pulled away after dropping Troy at his car.

After the movie, everything was closed, so they ended up going to TGI Friday's for something to eat. Bang had had the strangest feeling they were being followed since they'd left the Water Tower where they'd seen the movie. He blew it off, thinking it was just in his head. They ate and drank, leaving a little tipsy when they finally headed home.

They entered the Dan Ryan Expressway at Ontario. Pretty's head bobbed up and down in his lap until they exited at 159th and Pulaski. *Damn!* He couldn't wait to get her into the house to finish what she'd started. If there was one thing Pretty could do well, it was suck a dick. In fact, it was what had him sprung in the first place—since the night they'd smoked their first blunt together on her mom's back steps and she had gone down on him.

Bang had pulled up to the stop sign at the end of their street, still mesmerized by her remarkable skills, when out of nowhere, a silver SS Impala pulled alongside them and opened fire. Bang tried to pull off to escape the rapid gunfire but crashed into a second car that had pulled in front of him, blocking their path.

So many bullets had already gone into him that there was no hope; he was dead before the shooting stopped. Pretty sat slumped in her seat with gunshot wounds to her face and upper torso.

The two cars sped off into the night without a trace, leaving only the evidence of their evil deeds behind.

CHAPTER 12

THE MOOD AT Bang's funeral was somber. Bang lay peacefully in his casket dressed in a white linen suit with an ivory tie. The flower arrangements surrounding his casket were beautiful. Bang's mom, Mrs. Brown, sat looking at her son from the first pew, trying to remain strong. She knew the life he lived and the consequences of it. His father, Kevin Sr., had been a gambler who lived on the edge. One night, he'd won big in a dice game and had been followed home by robbers, who'd robbed and killed him in their driveway. Yeah, she had been through it all before, only this time it was her baby boy. And it was no easier to bear. Phil and Troy sat on either side of Mrs. Brown, attempting to console her as she silently wept.

"They killed my baby!" She spoke softly, just above a whisper, as she rocked back and forth.

The church was filled to its capacity. People stopped at the front row after viewing the deceased to offer condolences to the mother.

Soon, everyone was seated, and the preacher signaled the ushers to close the casket before delivering the eulogy.

"And God said, 'Let us make man in our own image.' Let's talk about that for a minute here. Let's talk about what image God had in mind when he created man in his own image. We know that God is spirit, because the

Bible says his spirit moved about the depths before he created the world. We know that he said he would pour out his spirit upon Jacob's seed. He says in the book of Joel, 'I will pour out my spirit upon all flesh.' And then in II Corinthians it says, 'Now the Lord is that Spirit.'

"The Bible also tells us that we must serve him in spirit and truth. Brother Kevin has gone on to serve the Lord in spirit and in truth." The pastor looked down from the pulpit above the now closed casket containing the shell of the young man the mourners had known as Bang. "Kevin was God's child. And now God has called him home. We weep and mourn because we feel that we have lost him. We feel as though he has been snatched away from us by death, as if death had somehow kidnapped him and now holds him hostage.

"Remember when we were little children, and it was time to go home and leave our friends for the day, and we'd cry? Our mama would say what? You'll see them again tomorrow, little Johnny or whatever she called you. She'd say, I'll bring you back to play tomorrow, right? Yeah she told you that she would bring you back! Well Jesus said, 'All that the Father has given me shall come to me'—not maybe they will come but *shall* come. And he would in no way cast them away, but he would rise them up on the last day.

"Here let me be a little clearer for those of you who don't get my drift. Kevin had to go home for now. But he's coming back to play tomorrow on that last day. So weep now, for the bible says it will endure for the night but that joy comes in the morning, on that morning when Kevin comes back to play."

The church erupted into amens and clapping hands as the choir began singing, "Please be patient with me. God is not through with me yet."

As if on cue, the bullets crept silently on the harmonic sounds of the choir from the rear, moving at Mach speed. One struck Phil in the center of his forehead, and two more traveled into the left side of his chest, leaving his lifeless body slumped right next to Mrs. Brown where she sat rocking. Troy snatched her to the floor. But it wasn't until the horrifying screams of the soloist rang out that everyone realized what had transpired.

The church was in an instant uproar as people raced to be first out to safety. In the end, all that was left were the two lifeless bodies of childhood friends who had been called in from play.

———◦◦◦◦———

"Brandi Rogers live here at Heaven's Gates Funeral Home, where, just a few hours ago, a mysterious shooting took place that left one man dead during the funeral services for Kevin Brown, the victim of a drive-by shooting nearly two weeks ago. The South Side man was gunned down in what Crestwood Police Chief characterized as a mob-style execution. Area 1 detectives believe it's a strong possibility that today's shooting is connected to the Kevin Brown murder.

"Earlier, I spoke with an eyewitness who declined to be interviewed on camera but did state that the word around the neighborhood was that the shooting was, in fact, connected to the Kevin Brown murder. He stated that it was believed to be in retaliation to a dispute of some kind before declining to comment further, saying it was a shame that it had all come to this and that the two men had grown up together. Brandi Rogers reporting live. Back to you now, Chuck."

"In other news, the Seventh Circuit Court of Appeals has ruled in favor of defendant Daniel Robertson this afternoon. Sandra Jones is live in the Loop at the Dirksen Federal Building for the reaction. Sandra—"

Rick pressed the mute button, returning to the yelling silence of his thoughts and replaying the horrific scene at his childhood friend's funeral. His mind kept returning to the conversation he'd had with his mother so many years ago. "Mama, why don't you like Phil and n'em no more?" He'd asked the question after being told he could no longer hang with them and that they were no longer welcome in their home. "It's not that I don't like them, baby," she'd told him. "I don't like the things they're into, and I just want better for you. That fast life they're trying to live ain't about nothing! It's just a fast trip to jail or the grave."

After high school, Rick had gone away to college at the demanding urge of his mother. So true was the cliché, "Mother knows best," he conceded as the old adage played and replayed in his mind, soon escaping the confines of his mental chamber out into the empty silence. He didn't know if he should feel happy, sad, or simply lucky he'd decided not to sit with Mrs. Brown where Phil and Troy had sat and where Phil had ultimately met his demise. Maybe it was a blessing he had been made to go off to school and had grown distant from his childhood buddies and their felonious behavior.

A tear rolled down his right cheek at the thought of how he'd wanted to sit with Mrs. Brown and the Crew. It was his place after all they had shared growing up. So much had happened between them; the bond they'd once shared that had made them so close and earned them the label the Crew was now nonexistent. Rick had briefly embraced Bang's mother after viewing his old friend's body as he made his way to one of the middle rows.

They had been friends in another life—separated by time and choices. His childhood friends had chosen the path that had ultimately led to their early deaths, while he'd focused on a more promising future. Although their friendship had ended a long time ago, Rick still felt a sense of sympathy and concern for them and their families. During his college years, when he came home on break and ran into their mothers in and around the neighborhood, they would always express how proud they were of him and how they wished their sons would get it together. He'd stopped hanging out with them when he came home because they seemed to resent the fact that he was trying to do something different with his life. There was always something to be said—something that questioned his blackness or the bravery of heart.

At first it hadn't bothered him. He'd shrugged it off, taking it as them busting his balls the way buddies did. But then one night, they were out on the block drinking, and he and Troy got into a tussle. Both Phil and Bang jumped in to help Troy. He didn't want to believe it had happened that way, but one of the neighbors caught it all on video, thinking it would be fun to watch later when they were cool again. To see the way they kicked and punched him like he was nothing to them really hurt him to the core. And it had revealed a truth he'd never forget.

After that, he'd started hanging out with his friends from college, going to parties and events hosted by members of the collegiate community. "The Crew!" he said to himself as he wiped away the tears, looking at a photo of the four of them when they were ten years old standing in front of his house, shirtless and barefoot.

"Hey, baby," Tanya said as she came through the front door of their apartment.

She and Rick had met in college and fallen in love almost instantly. They'd moved in right after graduating. Rick had proposed to her, and they planned to wed in June of the following year.

"Hey how was work?" he replied, trying not to sound as somber as he felt.

"Awe, babe. I heard what happened today at the funeral. It's been on all the news outlets and radio stations; it's all they've been talking about. I know that, although they weren't a part of your immediate circle anymore, they were still your childhood friends who once meant something to you. Care to talk about it, babe?" she said, picking up the obituary from the coffee table.

"Ain't really nothing to talk about. I quit hanging out with them fools a long time ago when I found out they didn't mean me any good. Besides, I should have seen it long before then when my mother said they were no good for me. I guess I was just too dumb back then though! No, babe, they weren't friends of mines. Nope, they were just some dudes I used to think I knew. Only went to give my condolences to Mrs. Brown anyway. It just hit me that it could have been me had I chosen to go down that same path with them fools, and it's fuckin me up! It could have easily been any of us that was up in that funeral home today that got shot because of those damn fools and the silly shit they were into!"

"No, babe. God is in total and complete control. It wasn't you or anyone else's time there today other than Phil's because that's the way God wanted it to be. God has something for you in this life, babe. And nothing is gonna happen to you before you accomplish what He has for you. Bang and Phil met their destinies, but that wasn't yours! All you and I, or anyone else for that matter, can do is pray that they were in Christ, that they had accepted him as their Lord and Savior at some point in their lives regardless of what they were into." Tanya said as she stood behind the recliner where Rick sat massaging his shoulders.

Tanya was a good woman—God-fearing with a heart of gold. Aside from her beauty and body, the fact that she believed so strongly in God was what had attracted him to her. She'd had her share of tragedy and trials, losing her parents and being raised by her aunt. Before Rick, all she had was her brother and cousins. She'd pledged AKA in her sophomore year, and her sorority sisters had become her new family—and targets of interest for her brother and his friends. They attended campus parties so frequently, they were thought to be students from neighboring Morehouse University. Tanya was always glad to see them in the dorms and parties, as they bought her any and everything, she thought she wanted.

Rick knew Tanya was right. His mom had told him as much only a week ago when Bang was murdered. "You're right, babe," he said. "It's just that, when death hits someone you know or, in my case, used to know, it reminds you just how fragile life really is—especially when it's someone your age or close to it."

"Yeah, babe. And that's all the more reason you should be thankful your mom raised you to have a relationship with the Lord."

CHAPTER 13

TROY WAS IN a silent panic as he looked over and saw Phil's head flop backward and to the side as the first bullet pierced the center of his forehead. Instincts caused him to grab Mrs. Brown and pull her to the ground underneath the pew. *What the fuck!* he thought as he retrieved the Glock 40 from the small of his back, checking to see where the assassin's bullets were coming from. He ordered two of his underlings to secure Mrs. Brown and make sure she got home safely. Not sure if any of his other members were among the injured, he swept the room with a slow glance from the floor, motioning to show those he could make eye contact with where he suspected the bullets had come from.

Making his way to the door by crawling beside the pews, Troy took a mental picture of the crowd in attendance and made an exit. Reaching his car, he dusted off the knees of his pants, glancing back at the entrance of the funeral home in time to see an older Jamaican-looking man dressed in a black suit hurrying away from the building as the police rushed in.

Who the fuck is that? he asked himself, jumping into his Cadillac STS and pulling off. They had stuck up so many people over the past few years that he couldn't be sure who the attack was coming from.

"Damn it, Phil!" he cursed as he descended the entrance ramp to the Dan Ryan Expressway, pulling out his cell phone.

"Aye Ray, dig. Get Bam and n'em and meet me at the tip out in Dolton!"

With all the dope and money, they'd secured drug houses all over the city and south suburbs and developed a following strong enough to take over the west suburbs as well. Money and guns brought power; the willingness to use them brought respect. They were known for putting in work in the streets without the slightest bit of hesitation. So naturally, they were feared by those aware of their reputation and followed loyally by their foot soldiers. Troy was a general to them, and Phil was treated with the respect of a prince by the gang members under their leadership. Heads would certainly roll in the coming days, weeks, and even months as Troy set his heart toward avenging Bang and Phil's murders.

"You have thirteen messages," the automated voice informed him.

"Aye, G, what the fuck!?"

"Bro, it's whateva! We out on the block. Get at us,"

"Bro, you cool? I just got word 'bout what happened. Hit me back, my nigga!"

"Troy, dis Mama. Call me, boy, when you get this message."

"Mr. Williams, this is Done Right Auto calling to let you know that your vehicle is ready. You can pick it up any time today before 7:00 p.m. We're closed tomorrow."

Troy's nerves were on edge as he sat listening to the voice mails and snorting the white powder, he and Phil had become so dependent on. He wasn't in the mood to talk to anyone. All that was on his mind was murder and revenge. He stood and began pacing impatiently, awaiting the arrival of the soldiers he'd summoned. Feeling the effects of the coke, he paced more earnestly, planning his next move with every step. For some reason, the coke always seemed to increase his ability to think and plan. Or at least that's what he told himself. He and Phil had become addicted to the white devil snorting it and lacing their weed with it, not long after robbing Tony. It quickly became the social norm of their inner circle.

"We hittin' all them muthfuckas!" Troy fumed to his young hit men.

"I know it was dem niggas J-Dawg n'em bitch ass! They killed one of the Bros, heads gotta roll, Bro! We at dem bitch-ass niggas!" one of the youngsters ranted, gripping an AK-47.

"I want dat nigga J-Dawg right here! Bring dat nigga to me tonight. And knock the rest of dem nigga's shit back on sight!" Troy ordered, dispersing his killing crew to the streets. He kept his main guys at his side to ride along with him for the night's activities.

Troy and his two killers pulled around to the rear of his girlfriend, Renee's, parent's house and into the garage before taking off on foot through the neighborhood. They stayed in the alleys, moving through the shadows and keeping close to the ground. They kept silent, moving at a steady pace, careful not to attract more attention than the barking dogs in various yards as they passed by. Barking dogs were so common in the hood that they often went unnoticed. Summertime in the city was full of sounds and smells—from children playing to police and emergency vehicle sirens wailing and from the sweet tantalizing aromas of barbecue on the grill to the nauseating fumes of fresh blood running down through the street drains. Yes, the city of Chicago most certainly was alive in the hot summer months, and the temperature was about to go up in degrees for the crowd of unsuspecting poor souls out enjoying the night's pleasures.

Two of the three-man killing squad emerged from the shadowed gangways in the center of the block in opposite directions, firing shots of death at anything and anyone moving. Screams of panic and pain followed the released bullets as they sought out fleshly targets to burrow through. The two shooters fired with a low, even aim, devoid of conscience or care, chopping down the unlucky attempting to escape.

At the sounds of gunfire and panicked screams, J-Dawg and his small army poured from a house in the middle of the block with thunderous claps from the deadly automatic equipment they possessed. They fired on Troy's men, hitting one multiple times and dropping him in the middle of his mission to maim and kill. Troy exploded from the gangway, letting the fully automatic MAC-11 disperse without restraint. He killed two of J-Dawg's top men before police sirens forced him to retreat.

CHAPTER 14

"HEWLETT PACKARD, TRINA Brighton speaking. How may I help you today?"

"Bitch, whatchu doin'?" Nee Nee said in response Trina's formal greeting.

"Look, hoe. Don't be calling my place of employment with that ghetto language," Trina said in a low, uppity white girl tone.

"Well fuck you then, bitch. I was just callin' tryna give you the latest word on the streets. But since I see you got yo ass all up on ya shouldas, I ain't tellin you shit. Bye, hoe!" Nee Nee spat back, pausing quietly as if she'd hung up.

"OK, OK, OK. Gimmie the scoop, tramp! … Nee Nee? … I know you ain't hung up on a—This tramp done, hon."

"Watch ya mouth now, hoe. I ain't but one tramp a day for ya!" Nee Nee said, making Trina laugh. "Naw, gurl, you get down there with dem white folks and get ta actin all brand new and shit. You 'bout to get yo ghetto pass revoked. I's shouldn't tells you shit cuz you's don't deserve ta know, Harpo!" Now she sounded like Oprah Winfrey's character in *The Color Purple*.

"Tramp, you know you missed your calling, don't you?" Trina said still laughing with tears in her eyes.

"Bitch I know that's the third tramp you done called me today!" Nee Nee said, faking a serious tone.

"Quit it and tell me, gurl. Gimmie the goods. Shit, you know I'm on these white folks' clock, and they don't play when it comes to their money."

"So a'ight, check dig," she began. "Camila comes into the shop today looking like the cat that ate the fuckin' canary and the last damn waffle with her plump ass. So I'm there thinkin this bitch must've didn't let go of the last damn Eggo or something this morning, and 'Dave the dope fiend shotting dope, who don't know the meaning of water nor soap', must've beat the shit out of her ass or something, you know?" Nee Nee said, laughing herself as Trina cracked up into the phone.

"You silly as hell girl. You are so wrong for that!" Trina continued laughing.

"Well, she may not have to worry about Dave's sell-a-bag, smoke-two no mo cuz some niggas came up through the block where they be hangin' at and sprayed they cockroach asses like raid! Word is that he might not make it."

"Awe that's so sad, gurl. And yo ass making jokes and shit. Got me laughing and carrying on. Not cool, gurl, not cool at all!"

"Don't be going all Mother Teresa on me, bitch, cuz it wasn't cool when dat nigga broke into my damn shop! And yeah I do know it was his ass b'fo you start. Hell, Cam fat ass was probably in on it with him. So boo you, and fuck him and them cuz ain't love trick!" Nee Nee said in a more serious tone.

———◦•◦◦•◦———

"Another brutal night across the city's South Side, leaving thirteen dead and five wounded when gunmen opened fire in the West Englewood area. Plus, the shocking sentence handed down to Alderman Jones and more. Fox 32 news at ten," the news commercial advertised.

"Oooh, babe, Nee Nee was telling me about Dave getting shot all up last night. They say he might not make it," Trina said to Danny as she channel surfed.

"Yeah I hear he ain't doing too good. His mama may have to get out that black dress," he responded, heading to the shower.

Five minutes later, Trina was joining him. She slowly and seductively slid the shower door open, stepping in one perfectly pedicured foot at a time. Danny just stood there watching her approach in slow motion. The steam seemed to give a mystical effect to the whole scene. He stroked his manhood, and she licked her lips as if she was savoring some sweet, tasty residue left behind by candy she'd devoured. He bent to kiss her, and she claimed his member as her own as their lips met and began rubbing it against her throbbing pearl tongue. He caressed her right breast as she forcefully pressed her softness against his tip.

He turned her around facing the back wall of the shower, and she assumed the position, placing her left foot atop the tub and bending over, exposing her juicy peach that seemed to smile back at him invitingly. He entered her and her sugar walls, and they turned to syrup, collapsing all around him.

"Ooooh, Dee!" she cooed trying to keep up with his rhythm as he long stroked her. In out in around out he went while reaching around and playing with her clitoris.

"Oh, oh, babe, I'm about to come!" she cried as Danny slowed his rhythmic stroke to a thick stirring motion, rolling as he pressed his body tight to hers as if they were merging into one flesh.

"Oooh shiiit, babe, you fuckin' the shit outta me! Get this puss. Oooh, I'm comin' again babe!" she cried as her body spasmed uncontrollably. All she could do to keep her balance was grab hold of the towel rack in front of her at the back of the shower.

CHAPTER 15

THE WAR BETWEEN the Bros and the Vikings swept through the city like a witch's broom, from set to set from the West Side to the far South Side in the Gardens. No one was off limits, day or night. The death toll continued to rise as the weeks and months went on. Rapid gunfire could be heard throughout the city from early morning to the wee hours of the night. Troy lay waiting in the darkness of J-Dawg mother's gangway for him to arrive. They knew he'd have a few of his men with him for security reasons, but the fully automatic Carbine-15s they were toting gave them little reason for concern.

"We got action!" Troy whispered as an old suburban approached and parked in front of the house. They rose to a crouching position and waited with fingers on their triggers and eyes trained on the SUV. Before any of the occupants could exit, the two masked men were upon the vehicle, engaging their assault. The rapid fire from the carbines sprayed equal rounds of lethal force to all, evenly dispersing death to everyone inside. So engrossed in the task at hand were they, neither of the two masked figures took notice of J-Dawg's approach from the rear of the house behind them.

Tricky went down first at the command of J-Dawg's Glock 27, never to rise again. Taking aim at Troy, he sought to render the same fate that his soldiers inside the bullet-riddled Suburban had succumb to. But his gun jammed, leaving him exposed and vulnerable.

Realizing what had taken place after seeing Tricky down where he lay motionless, Troy turned and fired as J-Dawg took flight into the darkness. Troy wanted to pursue him but thought better of it as he knelt to check Tricky for signs of life. He found none. Hearing sirens in the distance, he fled into the night.

News of the execution-style murders brought on deep fear in the community and a greater police presence. The Vikings struck back with vengeance in what police characterized as domestic terrorism, killing several of the Bros, as well as innocent bystanders, including a fourteen-year-old, when they opened fire from inside an ice cream truck as customers approached seeking the frozen treats.

While speculations of whether the feds or even the National Guard would be called in to assist in bringing the melee to an end were on the minds and lips of most Chicagoans, the Drug Enforcement Agency was before a federal judge securing Title III wiretaps on the Vikings street gang.

CHAPTER 16

RAIN POURED FROM the heavens nonstop, as if attempting to cleanse the city of all the blood that covered its streets following Bang's funeral. Credit for the hits had been given to the Vikings, and although they'd had nothing to do with it, they responded promptly when fired upon. All over the city the two factions performed war dances to deadly music played by their instruments of destruction.

Detective Jason Brown and his partner, Detective Keith Baines, sat in their unmarked car at the location of the latest shooting after walking through the crime scene.

"This is a fucking mess, JB!" Detective Baines said as they looked out at the bodies. "This is fucked up! A fourteen-year-old kid on his way home from school attempting to buy a fucking ice cream? Jesus fucking Christ, man!"

The chief of detectives was all over Homicide's ass to make arrests in the shootings that now plagued the city. Detectives Brown and Baines were Gang Crimes specialists and had a rolodex of informants across the city. They were nicknamed the Dynamic Duo in the precinct house over in the seventh district because they solved the tough cases and made the big arrests. In the streets, they were call Batman and Robin by the criminals.

Brown was the leader of a six-man team, calling all the shots. When it was all said and done, he answered only to the mayor and was basically given total freedom to run investigations the way he saw fit, as long as he delivered the results.

"It's time to bring the Vikings and Bros moneymaking operations to a halt. Get on the horn and have the team meet us back at the station house pronto, KB!" he instructed Baines as they steered away from the curb and out into traffic.

"A fourteen-year-old kid walking up to a fucking ice cream truck gets killed! He was a straight A student, Chief. That's just the first of what could potentially become many young victims if we don't get a hold of this thing. Let me do my job is all I ask. Give me the resources and manpower to bring an end to this madness!" Detective Brown pleaded with Chief Billings.

Brown had been in the chief's office every day for the past week requesting extra officers to assist in shutting down the two gang's drug operations. Sure, he and his crew could move as he saw fit, but he needed more manpower to implement the plan to perform simultaneous raids on corners and drug houses and a "no standing on the streets ban" on Tuesdays and Thursdays. All of which would require the chief's signature for the needed overtime.

"JB, you know as well as anyone that I want these lowlife scumbags off the streets just as bad as you do. I want them locked up never to be released. I got the fucking commissioner and mayor's heads so far up my ass right now that, when they Sneeze, I pass gas."

"Excuse me, sir. The deputy mayor is on line one." His secretary spoke through the intercom on his desk.

"See what I mean? Give me a sec here, JB. I gotta take this! No, no, stay. Don't leave. I want you in on this conversation," he said pressing the speaker button on the phone.

"Good morning, sir. Billings here."

"Good morning, Chief. How are you?"

"Fine, sir. I have here present with me Detective Jason Brown of Gang Crimes."

"Yes, yes. I'm familiar with Detective Brown. How's Jan and the kids, JB?"

"Everybody's fine, Deputy Mayor, sir. Just working to get these punks off the streets so the city will be safe again for all our families."

"Precisely my reason for calling. Please tell me you have at least one solid lead."

"Wish I could, sir. We believe this is a war between the Vikings and the Bros, all stemming from the murder of Kevin Brown, the young man killed in Crestwood a few months ago. He was apparently a member of the Bros."

"I see, well I'm not gonna mince words or bullshit you here. This is of the greatest importance to the mayor and the governor. The DEA has launched an investigation into the activities of the Vikings street gang. I want you and your unit to be a part of the joint task force conducting the surveyance. The special agent in charge will be contacting you in the next few hours. I need not remind you this is election year. And like I said, it's of great importance. The mayor wants to be able to stand before the city and tell them this nightmare is over. Give JB whatever he needs, Jeff!"

"Yes, sir. Thank you, sir!," Brown and Billings both said at the same time.

"Keep me posted. I want daily briefings!" Deputy Mayor O'Conner said before disconnecting the call.

"OK, JB, you have your extra manpower. Whatever else you need, let me know. Now get out there and get these lowlife pieces of shit off my streets!" Chief Billings said as he stood and removed his suit jacket from the back of his chair to leave.

CHAPTER 17

Spring 1999

TONY'S RECOVERY WAS slow but certain. It had been almost two years since the robbery, and he had completely bounced back. In fact, he was better than before. He now ran five miles every morning and worked out religiously. He sat at the breakfast counter drinking a glass of orange juice, allowing his body to cool down from his morning run before taking a shower. He rubbed the scar above his left eye that would forever be a reminder of that terrible night almost two years ago. He felt like he was marked with a scar of cowardice every time he looked into the mirror or even touched the place the bullet had entered his head. Even though the perpetrators of this stigma thrust upon him lay six feet underground, the memories of that night still haunted him. "This is bitch shit!" he thought aloud.

"Pardon, Senior Hernandez?" said Elise's housemaid, Maria.

"Pardona me. Yo no estuvo ablando con usted. Todo está bien," Tony replied apologetically.

Maria was very beautiful. She put most in mind of a younger version of Eva Longoria at first glance. She had been eighteen years old when she'd first come to work for Elise and Edwardo six years ago.

"¿Quieres algo de comer, Sr. Hernandez?" Maria asked, heading toward the refrigerator.

"No gracias Maria, y no tienes que llamame Sr. Hernandez por favor llamame. Tony said letting her know that she could call him by his first name, Antonio.

Tony had come to live with Elise and Edwardo in Colombia after being released from the hospital nearly a year and a half ago. When he'd first arrived and he could do little for himself, it was Maria who'd taken care of him. She'd helped him in and out of bed and fed him when he was too weak to feed himself. She'd even bathed and dressed him. Most afternoons, she'd pushed him out onto the grounds of the estate under the shade trees, where she would read the newspapers from the States to him until he drifted off into his afternoon nap and then watch him rest peacefully.

Maria had never been with a man in all her twenty-four years—never touched or even kissed. The desire to be touched had never entered her young mind until she'd met Antonio Hernandez and began to care for him. Now her young heart secretly burned for him and only him. She was uneasy and very nervous in his presence. She fantasized about how it would feel to have him make love to her every time she bathed or showered. Just the thought of him made her feel things she'd never felt below. And it made her so nervous, she continued calling him Senior Hernandez, despite his reminders to simply call him Antonio.

"Somebody has the hots for you," Elise sang as she walked into the kitchen. "And if you hurt that poor girl, Tony, what I'm gonna do to you has never been done to another human being in the history of the world!" she added, pointing the knife she was using to carve the apple she was eating.

"Nobody's gonna hurt that poor little girl, cuz nobody's even thinkin 'bout that poor little girl!" he said, mimicking his sister's voice.

"OK, but you've been warned, Antonio. And I don't sound nothing like that," Elise called as she turned and walked away.

CHAPTER 18

PRETTY FINISHED HER morning routine workout with five laps in the Olympic size pool on the estate she now resided in. It belonged to her newest sponsor, two-time champion MVP guard for the Los Angeles Lakers' Brian Cooper. They'd met over a year ago while they both were in physical rehab. Brian was rehabilitating a torn ACL. And Pretty, well Stephanie, was a victim of gang violence who was learning to use the muscles in her left arm again. She'd relocated to Los Angeles to live with her aunt after the traumatic encounter that had left boyfriend dead and her nearly paralyzed. Even with the wonderful work done by the surgeons at Northwestern Medical Center Chicago, she would forever wear the scars etched on the walls of her memory.

Sitting on the edge of the pool drying her hair and upper body, she replayed the events leading up to that awful night. She hated herself for having told Dee and Stank what she knew about the stickup that was done on Tony. She'd been given $20,000—that was what she'd gotten for the info and to convince Bang to take her out to the movies and dinner that night.

It wasn't supposed to happen the way it had. They were supposed to make it look like a robbery gone bad when Bang entered their apartment once they'd returned home that night. She would purposely forget something in the car and return to get it just as they approached the front door. The whole purpose in going out to the movies was to give them time to get into place in the apartment. It was clear now that the real plan all along had been to kill them both. *And for that, they would pay dearly!* she thought to herself.

Her cell phone rang, breaking her reverie and bringing her back to the here and now, where she was Stephanie Douglas, UCLA student with a major in journalism.

"Hey, babe. How's my man doing?" she cooed into the phone.

"Ah, a little sore from last night's game, baby. Did you check you out how I put it on them chumps in the third quarter?"

"You had 27 points in the third quarter alone, babe. Your stats for the night were 40 points, five rebounds, three steals, and two blocked shots! So now what do you think, babe? Was your woman on her job or what? I wouldn't have missed it for the world!"

"Yeah, you on top of ya game, baby. I must say, my lady was on her job checking for her man. You know, I really wish you'd come to some of the games with me though and represent in person, baby. I be wanting to look up there and see my beautiful lady cheering for me in the stands. Then afterward, I could be on top of you and you on top of me, if you feel what I'm saying, baby," replied BC, as they were now calling him in the media.

"I know, babe. And I will someday soon. It's just that, right now, I'm still a little camera shy, you know; and the scar is so ugly. I hate the way I look and how funny I move. It's embarrassing, babe. I thought you understood how I felt," she whined into the phone.

"Well, I tell you what baby. We'll be landing around seven tonight. Come pick me up and we'll have dinner together, just the two of us. I'll call Ralph and have him reserve the back room for us where it'll be just us and no one else—no cameras or nosy people to disturb us. It'll just be me and my beautiful queen," he suggested.

"That's cool, babe. I'll be there when you land tonight. I love you Babe!" she said before ending the call. *Yeah, Dee and Stank's asses are certainly gonna pay for trying to dead a bitch!* she thought to herself and smiled a wicked smile, heading to the shower to get ready for class.

Pretty dressed and headed out into the sunshine with revenge on her mind. Today she'd drive the convertible Mustang because she felt sexy and powerful. Although BC had a fleet of cars and money to burn, Pretty was no slouch herself, with nearly $300,000 her dead lover's, money tucked away. BC was so sprung though, he wouldn't let her pay a nickel for a sucker. And in her twisted, scandalous mind, that's exactly what he was to her—a trick ass sucker! She grinned and blew a kiss to herself in the mirror on the sun visor as she put her lip gloss on before pulling off.

Muah! Pretty kissed Brian as he slid into the passenger seat of the G-Wagen.

"Don't you wanna drive, babe?" she asked all whiny the way she tended to do when trying to get her way.

"Naw, I'ma just lay back and let my badass chick chauffer me for tonight," he replied, thinking how he was growing tired of the whole act. The pussy was good, and she did things with her mouth and tongue that no man could ever resist. For those reasons he kept her around and tolerated the bullshit.

"How was your day, babe?" he inquired as he reclined back in the passenger's seat.

"Oh my gawd! I thought my aunt Lettie was gonna drive me crazy. She called me like every fifteen minutes to talk about nothing. I'm telling you, nothing!" she began.

"She was just probably needing some of that Steph time, babe; that's all," he joked with a fake chuckle.

"No what she's needing is some dick, bae, real talk. I told you to let me hook her up with your uncle Jay. They'd be good together, I'm telling you!"

"OK, but if it blows up in your face, I ain't got nothing to do with it!" he said.

The next morning, Pretty sat in her aunt's kitchen sharing the details of her night with her cousin Sam. Sam was short for Samantha. She was an exact replica of Pretty, only darker.

"Gurl, you got poor BC's little head twisted and all fucked up! He done moved you up into his house. You got him having private meals made at the chateau and shit, shopping sprees and whatnot. Bitch you betta stop playing and go in for the kill on this nicca, cuz it sho don't last foreva!"

"Girl, a bitch like me done went in for the kill. You see how dis nicca keeps a bitch laced in the finest shit? You ain't know?" Pretty responded.

"You Chicago bitches are slow! If ya'll get any slower, y'all gonna stop completely! Listen, boo, it's not about what he buys you. Hell, you can buy all that shit and more yourself if you rape them pockets!"

"What ch'all chicken heads up in here talkin 'bout?" Sam's brother Junior said, walking into the kitchen.

"Not you, cuz!" Sam shot back sarcastically. "Look, I got some runs to make up on Crenshaw. Wanna ride with me, gurl?" she added, getting up to leave.

Since Pretty hadn't had the chance to respond to the "y'all-Chicago-bitches-is-slow" remark, she agreed to tag along. She reasoned it would give her the opportunity to check her cousin.

"Have a baby by this nicca?" Pretty interrupted. "Bitch, is you crazy? I ain't havin no baby foe dis nicca! I can see you ain't used to a bitch like me, cuz I ain't cut from that cloth. That's the dumbest shit I eva heard! *Get pregnant by a nicca for some money?* Look, boo boo, niccas get bitches knocked up all the time and don't do shit for the bitch or the baby. That's what you call going in? Bitch that's more like going out!" Pretty laughed good and hard. "I'd do better just snatchin' a nicca off the street and tellin' him to run it." She shook her head. "I thought you had the inside scoop to these Cali niccas, but I see you ain't got shit. Let a real bitch from the Gangsta Chi show y'all West Coast bitches how it's done," she finished, leaving Sam with a sour look on her face.

CHAPTER 19

DANNY COULDN'T WAIT to get to Pekin Federal Correctional Institution to get his father, who was finally being released after more than two decades. The lawyer, Mr. Randal, had called last night with the good news. *That was the best spent $150,000*, was all Danny had been able to think as the silent tears of joy and relief trekked his face upon receiving the news. Sitting in the prison's parking lot, Danny zoned out momentarily as his mother talked incessantly about everything from her garden to the neighbor's dog that barked at its own shadow at 2:00 a.m.

"You listening to me, Danny boy?" she said, bringing him back from his thoughts of the surprise trip he and Trina had planned for her. Now with his father coming home three weeks before the trip, it was definitely the works of the Father, he thought to himself.

"Yeah, I heard you Ma. The Jenkins has a dog that keeps you up at night, and you were thinking of planting some spinach or okra," he said, looking sympathetic.

"You are too much like your daddy, boy, you know that?" she said, reminiscing.

"There's pops right there coming out, Ma!" He hopped out of the truck.

Mrs. Robertson just sat there, frozen in the front seat staring at her son and husband, who looked as though they could be brothers embracing after winning the championship game in celebratory fashion. Tears welled up in her eyes as the reality of everything hit her. She was so used to seeing Daniel with the big beard. Seeing him now with it trimmed up neatly revealed just how young and well preserved he was. Suddenly, he was at her door, opening it and taking her into his arms. All she could do was cry. She cried for every lonely night of the past twenty years. She cried because he looked so damn much younger than she did and probably didn't find her desirable anymore.

Danny felt that his world was finally coming together. His new single "Don't Hate the Playa" was generating a good buzz. Calls from major labels A&Rs were beginning to ring his cell. He was done with the dope game, about to propose to Trina, and now his father was free. Everything felt like a dream he'd be soon snatched from, waking up to the harsh realities he'd sought to escape.

"I like this truck, son. This is just my style right here. What kind is it?" his dad asked as they drove away from the prison's parking lot.

"It's a Range Rover, Pops. And it's yours already—unless you want to trade it in for a newer model."

"Naw, son. I don't wanna take ya wheels. But I do wanna take it for a spin, maybe take your mother for a ride, you know."

"Pops, it's nothing. Me and Mom was just talkin 'bout me gettin you something to get around in on the way down to pick you up. Not only that, Pops, but we gonna get you some new threads as you call them too."

"Boy, you are too young to know about threads. What you know about threads?"

"I know plenty, Pops. I got you, old man. You ain't gotta worry 'bout nothin. As a matter of fact—and Trina's probably gonna kill me for not letting her share the news—but we're taking the two of you to the Bahamas in three weeks! Then after that, it's whateva and whereva you wanna go, old head!"

"The Bahamas?" his mother began. "Bahamas ain't no place for an old woman like me!"

"Baby, you ain't old," His father said, rubbing her thigh where they sat together in the back seat.

"Yeah, Ma, you ain't old at all, in case you ain't know.

<hr />

Danny walked the twenty thousand square feet that would soon become the home of D-Boy Studios and Production Company. Finally leaving the game alone and able to focus solely on legitimate business, he hit the ground running. A month ago, he'd proposed to Trina in the Bahamas and bought a house in Olympia Fields. At his father's urging, he purchased the land that would house his studio and production company in Calumet City, Illinois, near the Bishop Ford Expressway. The reasoning behind the purchase was that, since he was an artist himself, he'd always be going into someone's studio to make his music. So why not have his own? This way, he could turn a profit, charging other artists for studio time and get his production company off the ground at the same time—because he'd have the opportunity to observe new up-and-coming talent.

The studio was at the perfect location, close to a major artery of the city and neighboring states. No doubt with top-of-the-line equipment and a comfortable environment, platinum artists and up-and-coming artists alike would flock to it for its rich sound. In many cases, his father told him, artists traveled with their own engineers and producers looking to use studio equipment while on the road. Danny had a keen mind for business, so he understood how beneficial it could be to have his own studio and production company. He would have total freedom in making his music, and the money he charged other artists for studio time would replace his initial investment. With his father managing things, he was confident everything would be as it should. His father surprised him, not only with the major contacts he had accumulated over the years in prison but also with his vast knowledge and insight into the business and how things worked.

"Hey, Pops, I'm here at the site with the contractors going over some of the plans for the sound booths. Get at me when you get this message. It's concerning the pit and engineering rooms."

"What's up Dad?" Stank said as he approached Danny at the construction site, and they shook hands. Calling each other Dad was just a greeting slang they'd picked up from some of their buddies.

"Shit, Dad, tying up a few loose ends with this place. Trying to get the studio and everything ready. You know—business ready."

"I was with Tee last night, and he says you never come through to kick no more since your music shit been poppin' off."

It had been two and half years since Tony had been shot and nearly two years since the murders of Bang, Pretty, and Phil. With the score settled, Danny had washed his hands of the whole lifestyle. And as a result, he'd quit hanging out the way he used to. When Tony had returned to the States, Danny and Stank had thrown him one of the biggest parties street hustlers had ever seen. Failing to convince both Tony and Stank to leave the game alone and invest in the mortgage company he wanted to start, he distanced himself from his partners in crime. Stank and Danny would forever be close, but Danny stayed away from even the conversations surrounding drugs and the drug life and Stank respected that.

"Let me call this nigga foe he thinks I don't love 'im no mo!" Danny said, pulling out his cell. "Aye yo Tee. What's good, my nigga! Shit, here with Stank. Yeah, he told me what you said. You know it ain't neva like that, my nigga! Look we 'bout to go get something to eat. Won't you meet us out west at McAuturs in about thirty minutes."

Danny and Stank glided up the exit ramp from the Kennedy Expressway at Central in Stank's new 600 Coupe. Stank was the man now that Danny was out of the picture. He was doing well for himself and, at the same time, begging for destruction in Danny's opinion. Not wanting to appear as hating on his childhood buddy, Danny kept his thoughts and opinions to himself and kept the conversation light.

The three old crime partners hung out until around 7:00 p.m., when Danny had to part ways to meet up with his father to discuss business.

"What Chu getting into tonight, brah?" Stank asked as he pulled alongside Danny's black Infiniti Q45.

"I gotta meet up with Pops and the architect right now to go over the blueprints—something the contractors got a problem with, I guess. Why, what Chu on, my nigga?"

"Shit really. You know, it's Wednesday night, so all the hookas up at the 50 yard line doin' their steppin' thing."

"I'ma hit you when I get done and let you know what it is, Dad," Danny said as he gave Stank a dap and hopped out of the car.

CHAPTER 20

Summer 1999

"RICK, CONGRATULATIONS, BRUH! You're family now, Dad. Whateva you need just let a nigga know!" said a drunken Stank, bear-hugging his new brother-in-law.

"Yeah, fam. That goes double for me!" Danny chimed in. "I got some of my peeps I wanna introduce you to—that is, if it's cool with Mrs. Cordelle here," he added playfully, placing his arm around Rick's neck as he looked over at Tanya.

"Just bring him back in the same shape and condition he's in now, unharmed. I haven't had him for thirty minutes to myself yet," Tanya said with her hands on her hips.

Today she was the most beautiful bride to all who laid eyes on her. Stank and Danny had spared no expense on the wedding—from the horse and carriage entrance to the helicopter departure to the newlyweds' honeymoon in Italy.

Yes, today was certainly one for the record books; everything felt so surreal to Tanya and Rick as they sat at the table listening to their loved ones and friends making toast after toast to them. Her aunt Brenda's toast nearly brought tears to the eyes of everyone, when she spoke of the little brokenhearted girl, confused and afraid, as she waited for the return of her mommy and daddy that would never happen. Rick held his new bride close as they danced their first dance as husband and wife to Eric Benét and Tamia's "Spend My Life with You."

Later, they were whisked away by helicopter to O'Hare International Airport, where they set out for their honeymoon destination.

The weather was beautiful, and the sites were something right out of the movies. The food was rich, and the people were passionate and friendly. They met and old couple while in Florence who had been married for seventy years. They were in their eighties, still dancing and singing to one another and even writing little love notes to each other. In a world where everything was ever changing and always rushed, they'd never forgotten what was most important. They explained how they always made time for one another, loving each other throughout each day they were blessed to see together. Tanya cried listening to their beautiful love story.

Rick and Tanya borrowed their bicycle to go out and explore the tiny town. It was a double bicycle that was meant to be ridden by two lovers peddling through life. They road until the sun set, taking in all the beauty the city had to offer, stopping only to pick the beautiful flowers and take pictures.

The next day, they went to Venice, where they spent much of their time on the gondola rides touring the city. Holding each other, they were lost in their love and the wonders their eyes beheld.

———◦◦◦◦———

After the honeymoon, Rick settled back into work. The beautiful landscape of Italy was still fresh in his mind as new ideas for architecture designs flowed freely without end. Of all the structures, the Sistine Chapel was, by far, his favorite. All that was left of Julius Caesar's castle were a few pillars. But his mind ran wild with possibilities of what he could design based on what had once existed.

He'd launched an architecture design firm nearly a year ago, with hopes of taking the world by storm with his signature style and designs, but that had yet to materialize as of late. He sat at his desk maneuvering the mouse of his computer, trying different structure combinations of ancient Italy and antebellum to modern America.

The studio he'd designed for Danny was state of the art. There wasn't another like it; nor was there one that could even be compared. The concepts he introduced would, no doubt, be duplicated repeatedly because they were ingenious. He made it possible to capture every imaginable sound effect throughout the structure—the intimacy of a small, closed-in sound booth; a deep, down-in-the-pit rumble, or even the out-in-space otherworldly feel a hollowed room produces. He discovered how the atmospheric feel one sound had over another aided in achieving different producer's creative intentions.

"Cordelle Designs, this is Rick Cordelle," he said, answering the phone.

"Hey, Daddy. What are you up to?" Tanya asked.

"Hey, baby, just sitting here brainstorming, searching for that next big thing that's gonna change the game forever. What's up with you, wifey?"

"Aunt Brenda says that Grandma got the check today. It was for 5.5 million. She wants to meet later tonight at the house to discuss." There was a pause. "I guess she's gonna give Stank and me some."

"That's wonderful news, baby! After all this time, justice has finally prevailed."

"I know, bae. But it still doesn't feel like justice to me—like it don't seem real or right for some reason I can't even explain."

Rick could hear that she was on the brink of tears. Tanya was a crier to the tenth power and would cry when she was happy as well as when she was sad. He couldn't be certain why she was about to cry now, but he knew why he was on the verge of crying; and it had nothing to do with being sad. This was the break they needed, he wanted to interject, as he looked around his makeshift office in the basement of their home.

"This is terrific news, baby. We should celebrate! Come home, baby. Leave work early and let's celebrate together. I'll be right here with the champagne waiting buck naked just for you, baby!" He was attempting to divert the onslaught of tears and snot he knew she was about to start slinging.

"OK, bae," she sniffed. "And you betta be there buck naked when I get there too," she added in a totally different voice, sounding as if she was suppressing a giddy giggle.

CHAPTER 21

TONY PACED THE dayroom back and forth on the sixth-floor intake unit of the Metropolitan Correctional Center, commonly known as the MCC, filled with panic and cursing himself for being so stupid. How could he have not followed his first mind and just told Jeff's bitch ass he wasn't on right now? He had already promised those last two kilos to J-Dawg. But because Jeff was from Indiana, he could charge him $40,000 instead of the normal $38,000 for the two. *Fuckin greed!* he thought, pissed at himself, as he walked over to the phone corner.

"You will not be charged for this call. This is a prepaid call from … *Tony*, an inmate at a federal correctional institution. To accept, press five. To block any future calls from this person, press seven. To accept, press five."

"Tony! Babe, I've been calling your phone and paging you all night. What happened, babe?" Tracy said with desperation in her voice.

Tracy had been Tony's on-again, off-again girlfriend for the past three years. Their relationship always ended in disaster, but the sex was great. And Tony was addicted to her fellatio skills. He'd left her at his condo to go meet Jeff with the kilos of cocaine at Evergreen Plaza, where the feds had swarmed and arrested him.

It was a no-brainer that Jeff had set him up. He didn't even have to think about it. He'd pulled around the back of the shopping center, where alternative parking was provided at the rear of the stores, and parked right behind Carson Pirie Scott & Co., with plans to run into the Lark clothing store after the transaction and do a little shopping for him and Tracy. He wanted to surprise her with a few outfits and, at the same time, impress the chicks working as salesclerks inside the store.

The Lark had some of the prettiest chicks in the city working in their stores, selling clothes to the ballers with the slightest seductive suggestions. They were great at picking the outfits women liked to see on men. Tony would have them pick out a few outfits for Tracy as well because he'd found that there was something about a man shopping for a woman that was a turn-on to other women from his experience in other stores across the city. So it would be a win, win, win.

Instead, shit was all bad from the start, right when the nigga Jeff asked that stupid ass question. "Did you bring it?" Right then, he knew it was some sort of set up! Either this nigga was about to rob him, or he was wearing a wire. Tony wished for the prior, although it was no use now as he held the phone, trapped in the MCC.

"What does it sound like happened?" he said in an irritated tone.

"Look, don't be getting all funky with me. You shouldn't have taken your ass out of this house in the first place, I told you not to go! I said something just didn't feel right! So, what are you going to do now?"

"What the fuck do you mean what am I gonna do? I'm gonna have my lawyer get me a bond!"

"Unt-un, it doesn't work like that with the feds, babe. When my brother Red got arrested, they wanted him to cooperate before they would give him a bond. And when he refused, they gave him thirty years. Babe, you betta start thinking about saving yourself, cuz he sho wish he would have saved himself back then!"

"Cooperate? Bitch, what type of shit is you on? I don't even know why I called you. Who the fuck do you think I am?" *Click*, he hung up the phone.

After the second sleepless night, Tony was moved from the sixth floor to the nineteenth floor, which was a pretrial unit where he'd be housed until the completion of the case. The federal system was quite different than the state—not that he'd ever been to Cook County Jail before. But judging from the stories he'd been told, things seemed different. There were multiple TVs, an ice machine, a kitchen sink with a hot water spigot that produced 180-degree hot water for coffee, and even a microwave—all for inmate use. In a separate room there was a ping-pong table and lots of board games for recreational use. There was even an exercise bike and pull-up and dip bars to build muscles.

Tony kept to himself, not willing to talk to anyone, which really was not uncommon in these situations, as no one really knows who was who. It had even been said that Fed time is written in pencil, while State time is written in ink, meaning that Fed time could be shortened, while State time remained the same. The intake counselor had warned the inmates in the orientation speech not to discuss their cases with anyone because it could prove to be a big mistake. It was not unheard of for the federal prosecutor to plant a snitch on the unit to get close to someone they desperately wanted and to wear a wire on their person. Nor was it far-fetched for someone facing a lot of time to jump on another person's case. That was when a dude came into the jail bragging about how he was getting a lot of money or had killed someone and talked to the wrong person—who would then go and tells the prosecutor everything the loudmouth had said, plus whatever else the prosecutor wanted him to say, in exchange for a shorter sentence. Too many times, cats showed up for trial only to find the dude they'd been hanging with around the unit running their mouths to for the past year on the list of government witnesses about to testify against them. So, for a dude like Tony who nobody knew or recognized from anywhere, no one was lining up to say, "Hi. I'm so-and-so!"

His cellmate was a Nigerian cat named Abas. He was the only person to engage Tony in conversation, giving the new arrival the lay of the land and explaining how things worked, so to speak. He informed Tony of the mealtimes, lockdown times, the special census counts, and so on and let him use his extra Walkman radio so that he would be able to hear the TV.

After lockdown that night, the inmates settled into their cells for bed.

Abas wanted to continue communicating about what the city was like now and what was new. He had been locked up just over fourteen months, fighting his case, which was about to go to trial. Tony had no desire to talk about the place he had been abruptly snatched from or anything else as he lay on the top bunk looking out of the narrow window at the L train tracks that he never really took notice of during his time of freedom.

At first, he found no rest, shifting every few minutes and trying to find any comfort he could. Pleasantly satisfied by the light snore of Abas, he finally drifted off to sleep around 3:00 a.m. and dreamt of riding through the city in his new Cadillac truck until he was awakened by the sound of his name being called, along with several others, by the CO. "Hernandez, Anthony; Walker, James; Douglas, Brian; Taylor, Omar; and Lewis, Raymond!" the CO yelled again as Abas stepped through the door of their cell and informed Tony of his name being called for what was more than likely what they called a county run.

"Aye yo, celly, they calling you. I think they 'bout to pack you out to go to the county jail, man!"

"The county?" Tony repeated, still half-asleep and not fully understanding what that meant.

"Yeah, they got contracts with county jails outside the city, and some are even in nearby states, to house pretrial federal inmates. They be sending muthafuckas way out, even to Wisconsin and shit tryna break them down, so they'll just cop out or cooperate and rat on niggas!"

"They must have made a mistake, cuz I only been here three days," Tony said, swinging his legs over the edge of the bed to step down into the chair he'd placed beside the bed to get onto the top bunk.

"They don't give a damn about how long you've been her, brother. Some people never see this building. They go straight to those counties and only come here when it's time for trial to begin or to transfer to get sent to the joint!"

At a loss for words, Tony hopped down and went to the CO station in the middle of the dayroom. "You called Hernandez?" he said as he approached the CO, who was passing out large clear trash bags to the other inmates he'd called by name.

"Yep. Pack yo shit up! You are leaving, buddy!"

The scene was like something on TV when Tony reached the R&D floor. The expression on the faces of the inmates being shipped to county ranged from shock to confusion to despair. Tony really didn't know how to feel at the sight of it all as he was ushered into the holding tank.

The ride on the back of the van was something beyond Tony's understanding. Seven grown men sat shackled in leg irons and handcuffs, with belly chains further restricting the mobility of their already-bound hands. The entire back of the van was covered in thick sheet metal and steel mesh. Caged in like trapped dogs, they struggled to find minimum comfort for the two and a half hour-ride, assaulted by each bump they met in the road.

Tony couldn't contact his lawyer quick enough to set up the conference with the US attorney, after seeing what Doge County Jail had in store for him. He sat on the six-man pod looking in bewilderment at the setup of the jail, feeling like one of the animals on display at Brookfield Zoo. There were multiple cell blocks, referred to as pods across, beneath, and on either side of him—all with giant windows like they were on exhibit. It was as if they all had been abducted by aliens and taken to another planet, where they meant even less than nothing.

CHAPTER 22

Fall 1999

PRETTY SAT SIPPING her drink, looking down onto the crowed dance floor from one of the VIP sections of Club 213 in downtown Long Beach. She and her crew of dimes were on the prowl. It had been over a year since she'd seen BC. He'd disappeared like he'd just fallen off the face of the earth. One night, he'd gotten drunk and beat her up, leaving her hospitalized for a few days. When she was released from the hospital, it was he cousin Junior who'd picked her up and taken her to retrieve her things from the estate. He hadn't mentioned the events that had led to her being hospitalized or the whereabouts of BC, and neither had she.

Pretty thought long and hard after that night. She thought about how every man she'd encountered only wanted one thing—and too many times got it—while she, on the other hand, never quite got what she expected in return. The one exception was Bang, and that relationship had nearly cost her life. *Fuck that!* she thought to herself. *It's time to take it to these niccas. I'ma use what I got to get what I want!*

At that very moment, the idea of the Pussy Kat Klique was born, and she knew just how she would organize it. *First and foremost, only bad bitches, like myself,* she thought. *No mediocre hoes!* Her thought process continued. She knew her cousin Sam would be down without a doubt. "Shit'd fuckin these broke-ass fake ballers getting nothin' but a wet ass; her ass betta be down!" she mumbled aloud, just above a whisper. Then there were the other girls she'd met through Sam—Aliethia, Sharon, Tamera, and Jenny. The six of them hit the club scene partying until dawn every weekend anyway, so she was confident they would be down with her plan to make money.

"Look," Pretty began when she had all the girls assembled together, "I like dick just as much as the next bitch. But fun fuckin' a nicca just cuz he cute is for bird bitches! It's time to hit them pockets, ladies. And I got a surefire plan if y'all with me. Jenny, I know ya daddy got a lot of money. But I also know you got to be tired of jumping through fuckin' hoops for Daddy when you want something. And, Sharon, you basically got the same story with Uncle Big Bucks. And, Tamera, I've been that chick whose dude is makin' the chips and everything is his way or the highway; I've been you. Know that, when he gets tired of you, yo ass is history, and it's on to the next pretty bitch!" She went on with the proposal.

By the time she was finished, the Pussy Kat Klique was in full effect.

Basically, the way it would work was they'd target rich men to rob blind, draining their bank accounts and safes whenever possible. Once they had the account information, it was game on, and that was their main objective with every pump, stroke, and lick. Their preferred targets were married men because they made for the easiest marks, presenting the least trouble.

Sharon was a computer whiz; there was nothing she couldn't do with a computer. This was a very important part of their plan to emptying bank accounts from remote locations right under the noses of their victims. Next up was Jenny. She was a fourth-year finance major with an understanding of the banking system. She knew how to infiltrate the security systems banks used to move money in ways it was nearly impossible to track. Not to mention, she was a rich little white girl who no one would even take a second look or even bat an eye at when she was out swiping credit cards in stores or cashing cashier's checks. Aleithia was as slick as they came when it came to picking pockets. She and Sam used to hit the wealthy sections of LA together not too many years ago. Finally, there was Tamera, who's boyfriend's father was into movies. He was some kind of producer or such with a Rolodex of big-money types. Of course, getting their hands on it would be the real trick. But with a lineup like they had, they were very optimistic about the outcome.

Pretty was not new when it came to the streets. Coming from the mean streets of Chicago, she knew they would need some muscle and protection from time to time when things got a little stressed. She figured her cousin Junior and his Rollin 60's brothers could provide that for a small fee.

The way BC disappeared without a trace into thin air after putting his hands on her, she was more than sure they were up for the task. She had good reason to believe that Junior and his crew had their hands in his disappearance, seeing how they were all living high on the hog shortly afterward. She suspected they'd robbed and probably even killed him. Even so, she didn't care because, when Junior had taken her to get her things from the estate, she'd cleaned out the safe in the master bedroom, making herself $75,000 and a few chains and bracelets richer. She assumed the worst had happened to her former bae. But where she came from, the slogan went, "See ya, wouldn't wanna be ya!" And if you lived by it, you lived longer.

If there was one thing Pretty knew, it was niggas! She could spot a bankroll from a mile away and pick out the real ballers from the fakes just by their conversations and swagger. Tonight, the stars came out to party, she could see, as she caught the eye of Floyd entering the club with his entourage and waved to him seductively. *I ain't fuckin wit' you tonight, Floyd. Mama gotta get this paper!* she thought to herself as Jenny and Sam approached and flanked her on both sides.

They were occasional fuck buddies, she and Floyd. But she would never bring the game her clique played to him. She was his hole in the side pocket, and he was her always cued pick of stick. Besides the purpose of their being in attendance tonight was to see and be seen for a future encounter—unless, of course, the perfect opportunity presented itself. Otherwise, they were there mainly to create an attraction only.

CHAPTER 23

THE ATMOSPHERE IN prison was always one breath away from utter chaos. Hundreds of different minds meant hundreds of different personalities, which equated to thousands of different situations and scenarios. You got a crowd of dudes over in one section watching the game and cheering loudly or complaining, doing what's known as sweating tickets, which are bets they've placed on the game. Then you got the dudes at the poker table or playing dominos, chess, or any of the other card games and all that comes with them and their spectators. A few dudes are over in the corner doing push-ups, working out, and bouncing around like they're getting ready for a twelve-round bout. Then you had your TV watchers, fighting for control of the idiot box and what was gonna be watched each hour of every day. Whoever said that music influences were a very smart person. Since the introduction of cable television and music videos to the prison system, nothing had proven to be truer. Add the gangs into the mix, and the way today's hip-hop gangbangs through songs, and you have shit ready to pop off at any given second of every minute of the day. And that's before you even hit the rec yard.

Stank sat back analyzing all this from his perch at the top of the tier. He'd only been here for about eighteen months or so, though for some reason, he couldn't be sure. For the most part, he stayed to himself, only talking to a few of his homeboys. Although he was Brah, he declined to get on count with them.

Because he had taken his case to trial, he was not viewed as a snitch and, thus, could walk the yard without encountering problems from other inmates. In prison, you had to prove yourself by showing your paperwork—in other words, court documents—confirming that you didn't testify or rat on anyone. Otherwise, you were labeled "hot," meaning you cooperated with the government in some way. And if so, your homeboys usually made you go into segregation known as PC. In some cases, whoever had the proof that you cooperated could make you leave general population. Sometimes, tough guys refused to go to segregation when told and ended up getting beat up really bad or even stabbed and, sometimes, killed.

Stank looked around the dayroom and remembered once hearing that everyone was in his own world. Just the reality of it made him laugh almost out loud. He'd once been told that enlightenment was the silent acceptance of what is. And right now, it seemed he'd be receiving a constant stream of enlightenment for the next 360 months or thirty years.

He often found himself replaying the events of the last two years and how they'd ultimately led to his current life situation. Dee had broken away from the drug game clean and had really begun pursuing his passion, which was music. If only he'd quit back when Dee had, he wouldn't be trapped here in this madness.

"If the benefits don't outweigh the consequences, it's not a good deal, son," Mr. Robertson had once told him and Dee when they were at the studio. "The money is always good until everything goes bad. And with the feds, a black man will never get a fair shake no matter how much money he has!" He had continued with his warnings about the ills of the dope game.

Hindsight was always twenty-twenty. And looking back now, Stank could see it all so very clearly. Ah to God, how he wished he had taken the advice Mr. Robertson had given and gone to school for engineering. He'd be out there making the tracks Dee and his artists was rapping to instead of in prison feeling left out and shat on. It'd been said that situations don't make the man; they only reveal him. And right now, Stank was beginning to wonder what manner of man he was with the hidden thoughts he fought with that flooded his mind some nights when he lay on his bunk.

⋯⋯⋯

Stank awoke to the sound of his cell phone vibrating across the cocktail table. He'd dozed off watching an old episode of *Oz* sometime after Joy had left for work. He smiled a sigh of relief as he reached for it, knowing it had all just been a dream—or more like a nightmare that he was locked in hell.

"Yo!" he answered the angry device demanding his attention.

"Don't yo me! That's no way to greet your grandmother, now is it?"

"Sorry, Grandma. I just had the worst dream ever. I must have dozed off after Joy left for work this morning. The phone woke me up, and I just answered it without even thinking."

"Well dreams sometimes have profound meanings, baby. It's another way God warns us. I keep telling you and Joy that the two of you need to be in church."

"I know, Grandma. And I promise that we'll be there this Sunday!"

"OK now, baby. I'm gonna hold you to that. But more than me the good Lord is! Now, I called you to come take me to run a few errands today. I have to go downtown and to the doctor, and I need to get some groceries in this house."

"What time will you be ready, Grandma?"

"I'm ready right now, baby. I have to be downtown by 12:30 this afternoon and to the doctor by 3:45, the same time I told you over a week ago when you agreed to take me."

"Well it's 9:20 right now, Grandma. I'm gonna take a quick shower, and then I'll be on my way to get you before 10:00."

Stank hung up the phone with his grandmother and knew it was time for him to get out of the game. The dream had been so real he could smell the stench of the prison, and it scared the shit out of him like nothing ever had. Although he'd just recouped, a demanding voice in his head was screaming one thing and only one thing: *Get the fuck out!*

CHAPTER 24

TONY DROVE THE streets of downtown Chicago in search of a place to park near the Thompson Center, where he was to meet his attorney to discuss the purchase of land for the strip mall he planned to build in the Chatham area. Try as he may, he just couldn't stay away from the city he loved so much, regardless of the dangers or trouble it presented. He had, however, taken some of the advice Danny had given him. He'd moved into one of the high-rise condos on Upper Wacker Drive and was seeking more lucrative investments, instead of the run-down properties in the areas plagued with crime and violence, which was the purpose for the meeting he was to attend with his attorney, the lovely Loretta Kline today. His recent run-in with the feds had him hesitant to pursue the project, but his financial planner assured him that his investment would be safe.

Damn this a bad chick! he thought as he approached the entrance of the building, catching a glimpse of her through the glass revolving doors, where she stood dialing on her cell phone.

"I hope that's not me you're calling, although I would love to have you ring my phone, cuz if it were, that would mean I've kept you waiting. And it's not my practice to keep a beautiful woman such as yourself waiting."

"Good, because it's not my practice to be kept waiting, Mr. Hernandez.

How are you this morning?" she replied with a sexy smile that left him turned on.

Loretta Kline was bossy yet not bitchy, straight to the point but not arrogant or condescending. She was beautiful, polite, and professional, with no tolerance for bullshit.

"Well now that I've been chastised for the day, shall we proceed with the business at hand, Ms. Lady? I promise to be a good little boy."

"Children are chastised, Mr. Hernandez, and we can both agree that you're no little boy, I'm sure," she responded, giving him the once-over as she strolled toward the elevators.

"Well, I believe that was a very productive meeting with Councilman King, wouldn't you say, Mr. Hernandez? I look to hear a favorable word soon on this project. The preliminary drawings were very impressive. Who's the architect?"

"A friend of a friend. A young cat I was introduced to about a year ago just starting out trying to get his feet wet. He designed the music studio out in Calumet City not too long ago. Are you familiar with that project?"

"Yes, I think I am familiar with it. And yes, it's nicely structured."

"Forgive me for changing the subject. Can I take you to lunch? I mean the meeting did go well, and it was extremely long, right? You gotta eat at some point, so why not let ya newest best client treat you for doing such a great job."

"Yeah, I guess you got me there. I did do a phenomenal job, didn't I?" she said with a little girl smile.

"For sho!"

"I have a 4:00 appointment in Downers Grove. The traffic is going be a monster around that time, I'm sure. Rush hour! Let's go somewhere nearby or at least in that general direction," she suggested.

They ate at Bijon's, an indoor-outdoor café on Huron and Erie. Tony sat and wondered what it would be like if he could bag a chick like this with a real career. All the other women he'd dated always seemed to be on the fast track to nowhere. They were freeloaders riding on his coattails, chasing him for his money. Ms. Kline, on the other hand—or, rather, Loretta, as she'd instructed him to call her a few times during their conversation at lunch—was a total different breed, like from a whole different litter. She had his undivided attention, and he was on his best behavior.

"So, why is there no Mrs. Hernandez?"

"Why is there no Mr. Kline?" he countered without missing a beat. He'd figured out her game now, and he knew that her being an independent woman meant she was bossy to a point. But in reality, she was just sure of herself, and only a man with a strong confidence could hold her interest. Yeah, he was very familiar with the behavior she displayed, seeing it in his sister and mother.

All she could do was giggle like a little schoolgirl caught in her silly games and respond, "There is a Mr. Kline, he's my daddy!"

Something about Tony intrigued Loretta. Of course, she'd done some checking around and knew he was from the streets. And although she purposefully stayed away from street guys because of all the danger and drama that followed them, she couldn't seem to help herself from imagining him fucking her brains out doggy style in her spacious office as she looked out at the skyline.

"Well thank you for the lunch, Mr. Hernandez—I mean Tony," she said with another of her little giggles as she collected her things to leave.

"I hope I've been the perfect gentleman and shown you a good time. And if so, then please allow me to see you to your car," he said, flashing a mischievous smile.

CHAPTER 25

Summer 2000

TROY SAT IN his cranberry Jaguar at 75ᵗʰ Street waiting for the light to change when a brown box Chevy with tinted windows pulled alongside him. Troy saw the play unfolding from his passenger's side mirror as someone was creeping up from the rear. He remained calm, as if unaware of the jack move. Then as the guy appeared at the passenger door, Troy fired off five quick shots from the Glock 40 he'd retrieved from its hiding place in the console.

As the guy fell to the ground, Troy turned in time to catch another assailant getting out of the brown car and fired more shots, hitting him midway between the open car door and its interior.

The brown Chevy peeled off, running over its ex-passenger as Troy took off right behind it in hot pursuit, firing shots through the back windshield as his would-be assailants raced down 75ᵗʰ Street. Satisfied after seeing the car crash, Troy turned off at the next block and began his escape. Then with another thought, he stopped, jumped out, and jogged back to the wrecked car, where he found the driver slumped over the steering wheel but still alive. He wasted no time raising his gun and shooting the driver twice in the head. Tomorrow, he would drop the car off at the paint shop to change the color.

"Them bitch-ass niggas got to go!" he fumed as he walked through the door of the spot.

"What's up, bro?" one of the younger Bros asked.

Troy thought better than to answer and instead said, "Time to put some heads to bed!"

It had been more than two years since Phil and Bang had been killed and the war with the Vikings had kicked off. Things had finally died down, and money was flowing again. Tony had recently gotten back in touch with him, and he was eating good again. At first, Troy was suspicious of Tony when the call had come, not knowing whether Tony knew of his involvement in the robbery. But all suspicion was cast aside after the first five kilos arrived. Funny how greed can cause a person to throw caution to the wind. But it did just that all too often, and the consequences almost always outweighed the benefits.

Troy sat surrounded by his crew. Only those he considered to be his inner circle were allowed to be present during the plotting of their next move against the Vikings in response to last night's attack.

"I want them niggas outta the Dome tonight for good! Fuck whatever agreement they had with chief!" he said, looking at the room of killers. Although he couldn't be sure it was the Vikings who'd tried to kill him last night, but he couldn't be sure it wasn't. And he was ready for them to move out of his way anyway.

"We should burn down them niggas mama's houses. That way they ain't got no place to be holed up in the Dome no more!" Lil Polk proposed.

"That ain't a bad idea," Troy thought aloud.

"Aye, bro!" One of the runners stuck his head into the room. "There's been a van with tinted windows parked down two blocks facin' this way. Vee say it's got two Europes in it. Say they been there for about an hour now."

"Did y'all switch up everything over to the next block?" asked Paco.

"Yeah, we did that as soon as Vee drove down on us. I was just saying something cuz they still sitting down there."

Vee was Troy's cousin from down South. He'd come to Chicago on the run from the law and ended up getting high, smoking like a chimney. Troy let him live from crack house to crack house wherever he had drugs being sold. He called these houses "spots!" And as long as Vee kept them clean and did odd jobs around them, he was able to live in them a few days at a time.

In the meantime, he'd scavenged the neighborhood for other smokers and bring them to buy from Troy's workers. One of the odd jobs Vee performed was the walking of Troy's dogs. He had at least two dogs in every spot for security reasons. Like for instance in the middle of the night when his workers fell asleep, as they often did, the dogs were an alarm to them, alerting the presence of customers or any intruder.

On this particular morning, while out walking the dogs, he'd spotted the van with two white men inside watching their operation.

"Keep y'all eyes on and don't serve nobody y'all don't know—and absolutely no Europeans!" Troy said, sending the street hustler back out to grind. "This is the last thing a nigga needs right now," he said as he played the run of events in his head. "*Fuck!*" he exclaimed.

CHAPTER 26

TROY'S MEN SET out about the task of exterminating the Vikings from the neighborhood. Troy took a back seat to the diabolical plan he'd set into motion. Both he and his main five hitters would sit this one out and let the youngsters prove themselves. All in one night, their action would change the lives of so many, setting ablaze a sea of flames that would ultimately consume them as well.

Molotov cocktails would be used because of the damage and destruction they produced—for that reason, and simply because Troy had said so. They would strike at 3:30 a.m. because the streets were usually empty of witnesses at this time and, again, because Troy said so. Everything they did was to impress and or appease Troy. He was their general and commanding officer in this illegal war fought by two illegal make-believe armies—with real casualties and consequences.

Such was the gang life in Chicago. Nothing was what it seemed, nothing as it should be. Lives were changed or lost forever at the command of individuals whose best thinking often landed them and their subordinates in prison or the grave. What had begun as concerned members of a community coming together to stand up and protect it had soon become the poisonous venom that killed the hopes and dreams of the community it was formed to protect. This was not the thought of today—nor would it be tomorrow or the next—as Troy's young soldiers took to the streets in the wee hours to carry out their devilish misdeeds.

"Somebody got to die / If I got you got to go / Somebody got to die / Let the gun shots blow/ Somebody got to die / Nobody got to know that I killed yo ass in the mix bitch! Exchange hugs and pounds before the throw down / How it's gonna go down make this nigga go down / Slow down fuck all that planning shit / Let's just run up in they cribs make them cats abandon ship / See nigga like do ten-year bids / You miss the nigga you want and you murder innocent kids / Not I, one nigga's in my eye / and that's Jason ain't no slugs gone be wasted." The low sounds of the Notorious B.I.G. came though the speakers as the dark blue cargo van slowly drove through the block and parked around the corner.

JT glanced at Bam and Lil Polk through the rearview mirror in the darkness of the van behind him on the floor, where they sat lost in thought as he killed the music.

"Yeah, that's da shit right there, y'all lil niggas sleep on my nigga B.I.G.!" he said, shifting into park and turning around to face them.

They were all dressed in black from head to toe. They wore black leather driving gloves to be sure there would be fingerprints left behind in the stolen vehicle. Lil Polk and Bam each held backpacks that contained four Molotov cocktails sitting in MGD six-pack carrying cases to hold them steady as they made their way up the block.

JT quickly went over the plan again—for the hundredth time—and warned them that whoever wasn't back at the van within five minutes after they all stepped out was getting left. He had them synchronize their watches to his, to eliminate any mishaps—to the extent that he could.

All was quiet as they crept up the street. Only the howl of a lonely dog could be heard in the distance maybe two or three blocks away. Bam froze momentarily at the sudden sound of a car's engine coming to life a block over.

"Bring yo scary ass on, lil nigga. Let's get this shit taken care of so we can get the fuck on!" JT hissed, glancing back over his shoulder at Bam.

JT was the leader on this mission, the forerunner of the group, so to speak. He'd been on many of the missions the Bros did, putting in work

103

for the mob as they called it. Tonight, he was there to make sure Bam and Lil Polk took care of business and didn't fuck up.

The four houses to be hit were on the same block. Two sat side by side in the middle, while the others were near the end on opposite sides of the street. Their assignments had already been planned and discussed. Bam would throw the cocktails through the front windows of the two house that sat side by side, while Lil Polk and JT simultaneously took care of the other two. If all went according to plan, they should all arrive back to the van at the same time.

Bam was instructed to wait sixty seconds after Lil Polk and JT began sprinting toward the end of the block before throwing the first cocktail. This was a very important part of the plan JT had created. He'd drilled it into them over and over. It was to give him and Lil Polk time enough to get to their targets. But for some reason, Bam still threw the first cocktail in much less than sixty seconds. This left Lil Polk and JT exposed to any neighbor who may have been roused from sleep by the noise of shattering glass or screams that disrupted the peaceful silence of the night.

The plan was on its way to shit with this one idiotic move made by the youngster, JT thought to himself as he and Lil Polk increased their stride. Lights began popping on inside the houses along the block one by one as they passed, signaling that their evil presence was known. JT wanted to kill the youngster for the careless action because it seemed so deliberate and put him in jeopardy of losing his freedom. He was even more upset that Troy had seen fit to send him on what was beginning to look like a suicide mission.

They completed the job but not before finding themselves in another fucked predicament as they rounded the corner and found a patrol car sitting behind the stolen van, running the plates. They all slid to a halt and rerouted in the opposite direction, heading back the way they'd come at full speed. The patrolman must have gotten a call about the bombings moments later because, just as they'd made it halfway back up the block, they heard the squeal of the squad car's tires.

"Here!" JT hissed, leading the way through a gangway exiting the scene of heated action as the patrol car made the corner. Chicago was a city of gangways and alleys, where if you knew the landscape, they served as hidden trapdoors to quick escapes. They knew the hood well, every yard with a low or unlocked fence, as well as the ones without dogs, and it played in their favor as they disappeared into the night.

———◦◦◦◦———

"This shit stinks to high heaven, and it's only getting worst!" Detective Brown said, shaking his head as the paramedics rolled out the second gurney carrying a small, covered shape underneath the white sheet.

"So what do we know so far?" he questioned one of the uniformed officers guarding the crime scene.

"Jennings was the first to arrive. Said he was running plates on a dark blue cargo van parked on the side street here at 60th when the call came through. He observed three figures running through a gangway but didn't pursue because he heard screams. He was able to extract the residents of two of the homes. There was no one home at the thir—"

"And the fourth resident is where the two victims came out of," he interrupted.

"Yes, sir. That's correct. He was unsuccessful in rescuing them. An adult female and female child, possibly a mother and daughter, sir."

"Where's Jennings now?"

"In transit to Holy Cross to be treated for minor burns and smoke inhalation," the young patrolman responded.

"And the van?" he questioned.

"Came back hot. It was reported stolen from the Bucktown area yesterday," the other uniform answered.

"What do you think, JB?" Detective Baines asked as they made their way over to the stolen van.

"OK, so the van was the getaway vehicle, and then Officer Jennings shows up and fucks that up for them. They return to make their escape but sees the squad car and flee in the other direction, but Jennings doesn't give chase." He paused; brows furrowed. "I wonder what clues our mysterious friends have left behind." Detective Brown said more to himself than to his partner.

"I agree," Baines replied.

"Any prints?" Brown asked the forensic technician standing outside the driver's door dusting the handle and surrounding area.

"Just a partial that I suspect is too inconclusive to get a hit," the tech said, not bothering to break concentration with the task she was attending.

"Check the radio!" he said, unable to suppress his anger over not being given the slightest glance from her when he questioned her.

"Excuse me?" responded the tech, now laying eyes on the detective for the first time.

"Has anyone checked the damn radio? This model has a cassette player, doesn't it?" he fired.

"No!" she shot back, clearly angered by his tone.

"No what? No, this model doesn't come with a cassette player, or no one has thought to check it?"

"No one has checked it, Detective," she confessed, turning red from embarrassment.

"Do you mind?" asked Detective Baines as he pulled a pair of latex gloves out and stepped to the passenger side door.

Using his ballpoint pen, he pushed the tape door inward to reveal the back edge of a cassette tape. "Voilà!" he exclaimed, looking across at the forensic technician and JB.

Next, he leaned over toward the driver's side and touched the two exposed wires under the steering wheel, bringing the van to life, and pushed the eject button on the cassette player.

The technician quickly but carefully dusted the cassette, eager to be rid of the two detectives and their aggravating presence. "There's a full thumbprint here and what looks like a partial index," she announced, placing the cassette into a plastic evidence bag.

"Good deal. Let us know as soon as you get a hit back on that!" JB said, stepping away.

Later that day, they were informed by the crime lab that the prints had come back to a Justin Taylor. Homicide was already in hot pursuit of the perp, combing the neighborhood of his last known residence. After the call, JB and Baines rode down on their favorite informants and found out that Justin "JT" Taylor and Percy "Lil Polk" were running buddies and hung out on 57th and Wolcott. They took to the neighborhood in search of the two suspects, with mugshots posted on the dashboard.

The blocks were empty as they drove up and down them and understandably so, with Homicide and the detectives they called Batman and Robin circling every ten minutes. A known fact in every neighborhood of Chicago is that, when Homicide is around, you'd better not be!

It was hectic all through the town that entire week because they were harassing everyone they came across in the streets like old mean dogs in their hunt for JT and Lil Polk. Troy had already sent the two of them to hide out in Dolton, so they were nowhere in the neighborhood to be found. But just as sure as shit stinks, word of their whereabouts reached the ears of the neighborhood. And when the young cats attempting to pick up the scraps left behind by the shutting down of drug blocks began getting arrested by the police, they told what they'd heard in the hood.

CHAPTER 27

"TODAY THE DEA, in conjunction with state and local authorities conducted a sting on the Vikings street gang called Operation Fin Ball, arresting sixty-seven members on charges under the federal R.I.C.O statute. High-ranking members James 'J-Dawg' Humphries and Matthew 'Big Mack' Davis were among the arrested. The gang controlled a multimillion-dollar drug ring that extends from Mexico to the southwest side of Chicago. During the investigation, we uncovered an elaborate scheme of trafficking military-grade weapons throughout the Midwest. Many of these weapons have been linked to recent unsolved shootings and murders. Today was a first step in restoring peace to our streets. These are just the early stages of a catalyst that the mayor's office had set in motion to make Chicago a family-friendly city. Our message to gangbangers and drug dealers is a simple one: *NO MORE!* Leave our city, or we will take you down!"

Troy smiled at the news of his enemy's misfortune as he clicked from the news back to the Bulls and Knicks game. The Bulls were beating the Knicks 110 to 72 just five minutes into the fourth quarter. "Fuck with the bull, you get the horns!" he said in his best Al Pacino voice just as the doorbell rang.

"What up, bro!" Troy greeted Paco as he let him in.

"Shit, law. What Chu up to?"

"Shit, watching the Bulls punish the shit outta New York. You got some keef on you?" Troy asked.

"I got enough for a couple of Ls. Gotta tell you though, this is that shit on my mama!" Paco said, smiling as he held up the sandwich bag of marijuana.

"Twist that shit up then, bro! What Chu waitin' on? The Bulls doin' they thug thistle, and the Feds just snatched up J-Dawg n'em bitch asses and moved them outta the way for us!"

"I know dem niggas gotta be sick as a bitch!" Paco said, pulling out his cell phone to answer a call coming through. "What's crackin?

"Say what?" he said after a moment. "Wait a minute. Slow down, bro. I'm with G-Ball right now. OK just get a crystal clear drawin' and hit me back!" he instructed before ending the call.

"What's the demo, bro?" Troy asked immediately as Paco got off the phone.

"That was Bam. He say Homicide rode down on them and snatched up Lil Polk and JT. Darnell just took Lil Polk's ole girl to the station. He gonna call back when they find out what's what."

"Hit 'im back and tell him to tell Lil Polk's mom to let them know that he has a lawyer and that he on his way!" Troy ordered as he called the attorney he kept on retainer.

The news from the attorney wasn't good when he called Troy after leaving the 1st Precinct where the two were being held. "The statement Justin made is out there now. And all we can do is try to get it suppressed and preparation for trial, because they're gonna find probable cause, that is if they don't convene a grand jury to indict," the lawyer informed Troy.

"What about bond? Do you think you can get 'em a bond?"

"I gotta tell you, this thing is probably going to go federal really quick! We're talking about arson here, a federal offense to begin with. Then we got the issue of the mother and daughter that died. I think we should just sit tight and see what side this ends up on before we go up for a bond. Come down to my office tomorrow. We need to discuss strategy."

Less than a month after JT and Lil Polk had been arrested, the feds picked up the case just as the attorney had predicted. The two youngsters were transferred to the Metropolitan Correctional Center downtown on Van Buren Street. JT was already singing like one of the Temptations even though they weren't indicted yet. They were immediately separated upon entering the detention center to ensure they had no opportunity to corroborate stories. They communicated through the ventilation system and, whenever possible, at church services on Sundays when they could borrow someone else's ID card and sneak down to the chapel unsuspected. When neither plan worked, they left notes in one of the books in the library on a certain page.

Lil Polk sat on his bunk reading a letter JT had left for him earlier that day:

> "They talkin bout the death penalty, bro. I can't go out like that. I don't know about you. But it's deal time for me! I'm going across the street to the court building to holla at the prosecutor, bro. We should get our story together. What you going to do?"

Lil Polk was instantly angry at what he was reading. "Ole bitch-ass nigga!" he thought aloud. Here he was dealing with the same shit JT was. Plus, he was on the same floor with J-Dawg's brother Quan and a couple other Vikings by himself. The nature of the case alone was enough to make enemies out of strangers. Cases involving children had that kind of effect, even if you were a cool person. When the details of your case came out, a lot of people shied away from you or became instant enemies. Innocent until proven guilty went out of the window just as fast as it does for a black man standing in front of a white judge and jury. He made a plastic knife out of the comb he received in the hygiene packet they'd given him in R & D when he first arrived and prepared for whatever was coming his way.

Lil Polk had looked up to JT in the streets because he was always talking tough talk and had a reputation of being a real dude. Now he was acting like a little girl, Polk felt. His lawyer had also mentioned the death penalty talk the prosecutor was talking to him just a few hours ago, but he wasn't losing his courage and going to pieces like JT. His lawyer felt it

110

was all just talk to get them to cooperate and give them what they didn't have to make the case a slam dunk for the government.

"What's up, young blood?" said the old head with the raspy voice entering the cell he and JT shared. He had been the first person to welcome JT into his cell. He was from the same neighborhood, and at the moment, he seemed to be the only friend JT had in the whole world.

"Man, OG, I'on know. They talkin bout the death penalty and shit. I can't go out like that!"

"So what Chu gonna do then, young blood?"

"Man, OG, they don't even want me and my co-defendant! This shit ain't even about us! It's some bullshit. They don't even want us!"

"Sometimes you gotta make the sacrifice and take one for the team, young blood. It's just the way it is in this world, just the way it shakes out sometimes. Now don't get me wrong. I know you ain't tryna get the death penalty; nobody is. But they probably just talkin', tryna scare y'all right now. They gone bring a plea before too long," the old head encouraged, hoping JT would take the advice and not cooperate with the government.

"Yeah, well they betta hurry the fuck up with dat plea like you say, OG. Or, man, I'on know."

The old man slowly nodded as if to say he understood before getting up to leave the cell.

"Rooftop rec!" called the correctional officer from the dayroom.

Rooftop rec was just what it sounded like—recreation on the rooftop of the detention center. The entire roof of the building was caged in with a chain-link fence. It was equipped with a basketball rim, pull-up and dip bars, and a panoramic view of the downtown area for miles. Rec lasted for forty-five minutes per unit, and anyone was allowed to go with their unit when it was their turn. The only other recreation provided was in the gym, which was in the basement of the building. Because the MCC was inside a downtown high-rise building, there was no yard, just the rooftop and the gym.

Lil Polk was reluctant to go up to the roof, but JT's latest note stressed the importance of them talking. He decided to go because he knew JT had to have pulled some strings to get up there during another unit's rec time.

The moment Lil Polk stepped onto the elevator to go up to the rooftop, he knew something was wrong. Because the elevator could only hold so much weight, inmates were sent up in groups of seven to ten persons depending on the size of the average person in each group. He was in the last group to go up, which had three other inmates. The other inmates were J-Dawg's brother and two other Vikings. He didn't want to get on, but against the risk of showing fear, he stepped on with his back to the sidewall, where he could keep them all in sight.

The CO stepped off the elevator as if he was going to speak with the CO of the unit he was transporting to rooftop rec. The doors to the elevator closed. Bracing himself against the wall, Lil Polk reached for the knife he'd made from the comb. He kicked the first of them moving toward him just below the knee, breaking it with a loud snapping sound. He stabbed the second would-be attacker in the neck as he raced toward him with a knife of his own, catching Lil Polk in the forearm as he blocked it.

The third attacker, J-Dawg's brother, stood frozen at the sight of his two disabled cronies. Wasting no time, Lil Polk stomped down on the knee of the first attacker, causing him to scream out in pain and agony and never taking his eyes off J-Dawg's brother Quan, who remain paralyzed by fear in the corner.

The elevator doors opened, and Lil Polk stepped out into the sally port past the CO who'd left him to be butchered and beaten and back into the unit, where the other CO stood speechless before pressing his body alarm.

At that very moment, the entire detention center was thrown into chaos because another body alarm went off in a different location of the jail, followed by panicked screams of, "Code red. *Code red*!"

———◦◦◦———

JT had just finished talking to his girlfriend Tasha, letting her know she'd been approved to come visit. His counselor had called him up to his office and had given him the news just minutes before he went to call her. The fifteen minutes they spoke had gone by like seconds he thought as he made his way to the shower. He loved Tasha more than anything he could think of in this world right now. She was his everything, and he couldn't wait to see her. Just the news of her coming this weekend was enough to ease his mind of all the drama he was facing now, and all the mess he'd been hearing Lil Polk saying about him throughout the detention center. *Fuck dat nigga and Troy bitch ass too*, he thought as he grabbed the baby oil to take with him to the shower.

The water sprayed through the makeshift showerhead he'd made from an old plastic roll-on deodorant container in a forced manner—first cold and then slowly warming after running for a few seconds. He stepped into the little phone booth-like, sheet metaled cubicle under the water and pushed the button to keep the water flowing. The timer was set for about forty seconds, after which it shut off, and the button had to be pressed again. So every thirty seconds or so, he pressed the button. That was the system he'd come up with in the short time he'd been there. Another was taking a shower at this time of the day because no one really showered at this time, so he could have the entire shower room to himself and choose whichever shower he wanted. He chose the last shower at the back for the most privacy away from the dayroom.

After lathering head to toe once and rinsing off, he was ready to pleasure himself while imagining he was sliding inside Tasha. Reaching out from behind the shower curtain, he retrieved the baby oil he'd sat on the chair he brought into the shower room to hold his clothes and hygiene items. He squirted a nice amount onto his dick as he held it in his other hand and began spreading it, using the same motion he used to masturbate. Feeling the erotic stimulation, he sat the baby oil on the floor inside the shower, where he stood facing the splaying water, imagining it cascading down onto Tasha's back before producing unequivocal paradisiacal pleasure inside the both of them.

"*Oooh*, Tasha baby, this pussy is *sooo* good!" he said in a low voice as he felt himself about to ejaculate.

He paused and tensed his body while holding his breath, preventing himself from ejaculating, something he'd learned experimenting with himself. He pretended to hear Tasha begging him to put it back inside of her and told her to get on top and ride in a whisper only imaginary. Satisfied that he'd momentarily stopped the climax he was approaching, he once again began stroking himself.

Just as he was arriving at another climax, a hand reached through the curtains from behind, cuffing both his mouth and nose while another slit his throat.

CHAPTER 28

Spring 2001

AFTER THE ARREST and indictment of more than sixty Vikings, Troy took his drug operation underground moving through the city's sewer system. With his enemies removed and only law enforcement to be concerned with, he once again set out to build his drug empire.

The taking down of the Vikings created the perfect situation for him and his crew, who quickly moved in on the business left behind. The Vikings sold not only crack but also heroin. Heroin was always frowned upon by the Bros; they never sold it because they believed to do so was taboo. With all the money the Vikings were making off its sales, it wasn't long before Troy and his crew threw caution to the wind and jumped right in.

At first, they met resistance from the few remaining Vikings who were left behind by the Feds because they'd had no involvement with the operation. But they soon came around and joined forces with the Bros.

Troy was now the man in the city and loving every minute of it. He and Tony were extremely close, clubbing almost every weekend. He plugged Tony with the head leader of the Bros, and the three of them hung out on Sunday afternoons and shot ball with the city's elite—like

MJ, Scottie, Randy, and occasionally RK when he was in town—over at the LeClair Courts Recreational Center. It was nothing for them to shoot around before and after games, making $25,000 bets on single jump shots. Tony introduced Troy to a new life, a world he never knew existed. They ate at the best restaurants, wore the best clothes, and enjoyed only the finest life had to offer.

"Yo, what it do, my nigga? What you up to? Where ya at?" Tony said when Troy answered.

"Pickin up TJ from day care. What's good, my nigga?"

TJ was Troy's son by Renee. Although he and Renee were no longer together, Troy took care of her and spent time with Troy Jr. daily. His every weekday routine was picking up TJ from daycare and taking him to McDonald's and then to his mother's house to spend time with Grandma until Renee got off work and came to get him.

"Aye, I'm at the doghouse. I got cha girl Cobra and Sunshine n'em down here ready to do something strange for that change!"

"Nigga, yo ole freak leg ass," Troy said, laughing. "Naw, my nigga. I'm cool," he added. "Me and my lil man 'bout to hang out for the day. 'Bout to take him to get a haircut and then to the mall." TJ was Troy's world, and nothing else in life meant more to him.

"A'ight then, my dude. Slide through when you come to the crib though," Tony said, ending the call. They had condos in the same building and called Tony's place the doghouse because it's where they dogged out chicks.

Troy hung up, shaking his head, and laughing to himself as he thought about what Tony probably had them down there doing.

———

"So, you saying that that nigga Ty is broke and tryna sell Factory 303?" Troy said as they drove up Michigan Avenue in Tony's Bentley on their way to the jeweler.

Factory 303 was a club located in the South Loop that had once been one of the city's premiere hot spots until it just fizzled out.

"Yeah, he called me last night. The nigga says he tryna get like

$150,000 for it. You know, it ain't been doing too good since them people died up there the other year. I figure we could go half on it and do the damn thang, my nigga!"

"Man, let me think 'bout this a couple days."

"Nigga, what's to think about? We put up the money and shit and make it right back in the first couple of months! Trust me, nigga; if I tell you it's cheese on the moon, take some crackers. On the serious side, though, I got my lawyer checkin' shit out. If shit checks out good, it's a go for me. I was just giving you an opportunity to get in on it. You need some legit shit, nigga. I don't know what the fuck you be thinkin'."

"Yeah, you right, my nigga. A nigga do need something on the up-and-up, you ain't never lied! If it checks out, I got my seventy-five."

"Aye yo, you know it's Black Biker Week coming up next month. What Chu gone do? You riding or what?" Tony asked, switching subjects.

"Nigga, if it's all you niggas make it out to be, bad bitches everywhere just tryna fuck and suck something, hell yeah. Why wouldn't I?" Troy said, getting excited just imagining the scene.

"I'm for real, nigga!" Troy added, thinking Tony—who'd just burst out into laughter out of nowhere—was laughing at his response.

"Naw, I was just thinkin' 'bout when you went and bought that lil ass 600, and we went riding," Tony could barely say for laughing too hard. "Nigga, you's a fool for real," he managed to get out in between breaths.

Tony had tried to convince Troy to get a bigger and more powerful bike—like at least a 1000 or 1100—something worth the money. All that had gone in one ear and out the other; the very next day, Troy rode up on a shiny new 600. Tony and the other guys he rode with fell out laughing and couldn't wait to take off riding. At that very moment, Troy didn't know he was the target of their laughter. But he did later that night when they were sitting around drinking at Hard Rock Café.

Earlier that day, they had been out on Lake Shore Drive all doing upward of a 100 mph when a state trooper got behind them. Everybody got away but Troy, so the trooper gladly gave him twelve tickets, one for everyone who'd gotten away, plus his own. The next week, he showed up on a new 1300 Busa—lesson learned!

"Nigga, fuck you!" Troy said, laughing at himself.

Black Biker Week was a three-day event located in Myrtle Beach, South Carolina, where black motorcycle clubs from all over the United States convened to hang out and party hearty from May 22 through May 25. Although the event was only scheduled for the three days, it began early with the arrivals of the early birds and ended with the stragglers departing a day or two late.

Tony and Troy would be riding down with the Nighthawks of Chicago motorcycle club. The president of the club was a friend of Tony's from the west side named Cat Eyes. He agreed to let Tony and Troy ride along with them, if they respected the formation of travel when riding and wore helmets in accordance with the law to avoid any hassle. The trip was 821 miles from Chicago. The planned route was through Indiana, up to I-26 East in Tennessee, which would take them on into South Carolina, Cat Eyes explained in case they fell behind somehow. Motorcycle clubs, they would come to see, were really organized and structured like that.

CHAPTER 29

"FUNERAL OF AN old pal / Back then in a million years we couldn't have pictured now / It seemed we'd live forever stranded in the crowd / Lights cameras but ain't no action round here now," Danny recited, laying the first verse of a new song called "R.I.P. Homie"

"Aye, let me hear that back," he said to Stank, who was working the boards in the engineering room.

Stank had been attending Columbia College downtown in the Loop learning the art of studio engineering. The past year had been nothing short of spectacular. Danny's freshmen album, *The Life of a Playa*, had gone double platinum and was still selling. He was tapped to perform at the BET Awards, the MTV Awards, and the Soul Train Music Awards, all this year. His music was everywhere. You couldn't pull up to any stoplight or turn on the radio without hearing one of his songs. His schedule was mad crazy with all the TV and radio appearances and interviews. Then there were the shows. It seemed like every concert promoter in the country wanted him at a venue in their city. Currently, he was working on his sophomore album *Return to the Scene* and had five collaborations for the project already underway. The first of the five was "R.I.P. Homie", a song he was doing with Scarface in dedication to their fallen comrades.

"Aye yo turn me up just a little bit and take the violins down some," he told Stank as they rode, listening to the verse he'd just laid on their way to get something to eat. "I feel like this album is gone do even better than the last. I'm looking for some crazy numbers, you feel me?" he continued.

"Yeah, the first one did like, what, 200,000 units in the first week, didn't it? Then with Face and Jay and Yay on this shit—I ain't even gone mention Jada Common, & Project Pat—this muthafucka is a banga!" Stank said excitedly.

"Yeah, I do feel good about it. But repeating the success is the toughest part of this business so I hear."

They returned to the studio to find Trina and the kids in studio B where they had been working. "Hey, is that daddy's girl?" Danny said, sneaking up behind his daughter and snatching her up into the air from where she stood watching her big brother play with the knobs and levels on the board.

"Hey, baby, what a pleasant surprise!" he said sarcastically as he bent to kiss her, taking his son from her and holding him up in the air.

"What's up with daddy's little man? How's daddy's boss man?"

"Yeah, we figured we'd pop in on ya for a quick second on our way to take Heaven to dance and Lil Jay to the dojo," she said, standing beside him and looking up at him and their son.

"If this little girl comes and gets me one more time to watch that video! Oh and she ain't letting you leave until it goes off I'm telling you," Trina said, sounding exasperated.

"Yeah, Dad. it hit number one on 106 & Park countdown!" Jay said, stepping away from the boards and finally acknowledging his dad's presence.

"Well give me some dap then, son, and let me know you recognize ya old man doing his thang!" Danny said fist-bumping with Jay.

"Always give a dude his props when he got 'em coming," he added with his arm draped around his son's shoulder, looking down at him.

"What props, Dad?" Jay asked, confused.

"Props is short for proper recognition, like when you do good at the dojo and receive a new color belt to show it. That says to everyone who sees it, 'I did that!'" He explained the way he always did, taking time out to break things down like a wise and patient father.

"The instructor at the dojo, Mr. Cooper, says that Jay is one of his best students!" Trina said, beaming with pride for her firstborn.

"OK, that's what I'm talkin 'bout, son. Give me some!" Danny said, holding out his fist for Jay to bump again.

"Yeah, Dad. Give me my props!"

"Ah the boy sharp right here!" Stank said, high-fiving Trina.

"That's my little man!" she said draping her arm over his shoulder.

"It's a go, baby—ten city tour. Daddy gotta get out there and get this money!" Danny said excitedly as he hung up the phone.

"Yeah, but you just got back not even a week ago, bae!" Trina said, pouting.

"Awe, babe. Come here," he said, pulling her into his lap. "Listen, babe. You know everything I do, I do for you and the kids, tryna give y'all the best life has to offer. I mean I know I'm gone a lot right now, but I promise you it won't be like this always!"

It was true that Danny was hardly ever home these days. Even when he wasn't out on the road, he was holed up in the studio working on something for the next album that would ultimately take him back out on the road. To him, it seemed like living a legitimate lifestyle was more stressful somehow than his previous illegal world had been—although the benefits were far greater.

Trina remained silent with her lips poked out like their daughter, little Heaven.

"Tell you what. When I get back from this tour, we'll take a nice long vacation. We'll take the kids down to Disney World, and then we'll go wherever the wind blows our sails," he said, lifting her chin and looking into her eyes.

"K," she replied, pouty just like little Heaven would.

CHAPTER 30

TROY NOTICED THE increased motorcycle traffic as they entered South Carolina. The atmosphere was crazy! The culture was kaleidoscopic to say the least, with bikers from all walks of life making their way to meet in the same city. He felt the excitement in the air the closer they got. They swarmed into the parking lot of the hotel where they had reservations only blocks from the beach. There were all female motorcycle clubs, with beautiful chicks on pink, purple, red, and yellow Ducati and Busa like Troy's in all leather pants and bikini tops.

"This shit is insane!" Troy said to Tony as they parked their bikes.

"You ain't seen nothin yet. Wait till we hit the beach, my nigga. It's gone be like we at Spring Bling! Nothing but badass bitches out there just dyin' to fuck a nigga!" Tony said, kicking down his kickstand and getting off his bike.

"Look at that country as shit!" Cat Eyes said as he passed by going to the dually truck they brought along on trips in case someone's bike broke down and needed to be put on the trailer attached. New pledges to the club were tasked with driving the dually and pulled their bikes on the trailer until they were granted membership and earned their place in the riding formation.

"What the fuck is that?" Troy asked, laughing.

"A furred-out Gixxer," Cat Eyes shot back over his shoulder as he continued his way.

Nothing could have prepared Troy for what he saw as they approached the beach. There were three women to every one man literally, and these were some of the badest chicks he had ever laid eyes on. They'd left their bikes and gone at it on foot because the streets were jam-packed everywhere they went. Traffic was so backed up that the roads looked like a giant parking lot. Guys and girls were grouped up in different groups smoking weed and drinking, with music blaring all around from different cars and trucks. Daredevil cats popped wheelies and did tricks up and down the shoulder of the road for short stretches, trying to outdo one another while impressing the beautiful women spectating. Everywhere he looked, there was something different going on. Twerking contests on the roof and hoods of cars. Chicks flashed their boobs, shaking them wildly out of car windows. You name it, and it was going on right there in the streets in the middle of everything and everybody.

Troy stepped behind this fine thick stallion of a women dancing with her friends, Chicago jacking as if they were on the dance floor in a club. She quickly obliged, bending all the way over and throwing her ass backward into his crotch, while her girls surrounded him, jacking on him in the same fashion he was jacking on her. Tony wasted no time joining in on the fun. After all the drinks, weed, and ex pills, the rest of the night was a blur.

The next morning, Troy woke up with three of the six-woman crew in his hotel bed. Two lay at both his sides, with the third between his legs with her head on his abdomen. Before parting to catch up with Tony, he gave them each $500 and told them that their outfits for the day were on him.

"Man, last night was wild!" Tony said as Troy approached and sat on his bike.

"I'll tell you what," Troy began. "We gotta slide up through Tennessee if they dimes like last night getting down like that."

Both laughed as they high fived.

"Yeah, my nigga, them bitches was so tough I had to give em a nickel each and told them to buy 'em somethin' nice on me!"

Troy laughed and said, "I did the same thing, my nigga! On my mama, I did the same muthafuckin' thing!"

The pair were laughing again.

"Aye, D-boy is performing today at that shit they havin' on the beach. He hit me up and said we should come hang out before they head out. You know he's on tour right now," Tony said, starting his bike.

"Yeah? You know that nigga like that?" Troy asked.

"Do I? Danny Boy is like my brother. We go way back!"

"Oh, that's what's up then," Troy said. As he turned the ignition key, he thought about how he regretted his role in the robbery, wishing he could go back in time.

Tony was cool people, like he'd tried explaining to Phil. They all could have gotten money with him. But Phil had been so hell-bent on taking his shit. Sure, he had set it all up. But had he known Tony the way he did now, he wouldn't have ever mentioned his name to Phil in the first place. And most certainly, he wouldn't have shot him.

CHAPTER 31

"MAN, POPS, THIS music business ain't no joke! I can't even remember the last time I had a home-cooked meal or slept in my own bed," Danny said to his father, looking out the window of his tour bus.

"This is what you signed up for, son. This is your dream. And only you can engraft that which brings you happiness. But first you must decide what makes you happy and then find the balance between what it brings and what it takes away. That's the thing right there, because happiness is being content with what you have, not what you don't."

"Damn, Mr. Robertson, that was deep!" Stank said, taking a bite from his apple.

"Not nearly as deep as you think, son. It's just the truth of the matter," Mustafa replied.

"He's just gone off that hydro, Pops. That's why he keeps callin' you Mr. Robertson and shit. He does that every time he's high," Danny said, and they all began laughing.

"Yeah, that's it though, Pops. Like you said, I gotta find that balance. You hit it right on the head, cuz I love what I do and where it's goin. But ain't nothing more important to me than Trina and the kids! When I told her about this ten-city tour, I was all excited, but she looked like she'd just gotten some bad news. That's when it hit me, I'd just gotten back from Cali not even a week ago, and I'd been in the studio day in and day out working on this next album, and now I'm 'bout to be gone again," Danny said, pouring himself a shot of Rémy XO. "I'm takin' her and the kids to Disney World for a couple of weeks after this tour. Then we're gonna go someplace for another week or two without the kids. Don't schedule nothing for me before July."

"Sounds good to me, son," his father said. "VH1 wants to start taping for the reality show the last week of July / early August. How does that sound to you? It should give you time to get back and get settled into things."

"That's cool. Let's make sure we don't set that in July at all, Pops."

"Stank, what time is sound check for Myrtle Beach?" Danny asked.

"Uh, like seven in the morning I believe," Stank said reaching for the itinerary. "Yep, 7:00 a.m.," he confirmed before tossing the folder back onto the table.

"Well, I'm turning in. AJ says we should be pullin' into Myrtle Beach around 5:00 a.m., and that's only two hours before sound check," Danny said, heading farther into the tour bus.

Danny lay with the blinds cracked slightly staring out at the road in more of a review than a daydream. Everything was happening so fast right before his eyes. It was like all his dreams were being placed at his fingertips and all he had to do was grab ahold of them. But the more he tightened the grip of that hand, it seemed to ease the grip of the other hand holding onto his family. He loved his family without a doubt. But the pursuit of his dreams somehow seemed to contradict or abate that one simple truth, leaving him feeling torn and dejected at moments like this. It was as if every step closer to success in his music career was met by one equal step away from Trina and the kids. He'd make it right, he thought as he drifted off to sleep—somehow, some way.

Danny performed one-verse snippets of four songs and "Don't Hate the Playa" in its entirety because it was currently number one in the country. Everyone knew the words, and most of the crowd sang along. He brought Tony and Troy up on stage, along with about seven females from the audience, as props when he performed the hit. It was a suggestion his father had made, and it worked out perfectly.

"Nigga, you did that!" Stank said as they exited the stage with the crowd still going wild.

"Naw, brah, *we did that*!" he responded, smiling at Stank.

"Great show, son!" his father said, giving him a nod of approval.

"Yeah, my nigga. I'ma have to get you to write me a few verses if this is how the ladies react when a nigga rap!" Tony said, listening to the crowd chanting "D-Boy, D-Boy!" as various women screamed out, "I love you, D-Boy!"

"You sure you want that? because a lot of them broads be crazy as hell," Danny jokingly replied as they headed for the bus.

"We got some catchin' up to do, my nigga. I ain't seen you since Stank's sister's wedding. What Chu got goin' on, playboy?" Tony said as they sat in Danny's tour bus.

"Man, it's been mad hectic. Right now, I got this ten-city tour starting tomorrow. Then I'm 'bout to do a reality show with VH1 called *Dee Life*—you know, like 'thee' but it's 'Dee' instead. Let me see, just got done taping for the MTV Awards out in Cali. Still got the BET Awards and the Soul Train Awards coming up later this year. Man, it's been work, work, work! I ain't even been on my job at the crib, brah. So, you already know I'm in the doghouse 'bout that."

"Yeah, you know I know Trina ain't goin' for none of that! I know she been trippin' like a mutha on you and shit my nigga," Tony said, putting extra emphasis on the word "mutha" as he raised his eyebrows, slowly shaking his head.

"What's been up with you though, brah?" Danny asked.

"You know, I'm building that strip mall over on Cottage Grove, just waiting for the green light from the city to break ground. Shit, they more crooked down at city hall than niggas are in the streets! The muthafuckas are some gangstas for real, baby boy. You gotta pay to play down there, no doubt!" Tony said, pausing to sip his drink. "Then I'm probably gonna buy this club from South Side Ty if my lawyer says everything checks out."

"Factory 303?" Danny asked.

"Yeah, I'll probably change the name to something with a better feel to it—something sexy that'll make bitches wanna take off their clothes and shit!" He laughed but more to himself.

"Naw, but seriously though, I might change it to something with more appeal. Lately though, I been just enjoying life, lovin' every minute of it."

"How's your mom and Elise? I gotta call and say hi!"

"Yeah, they cool. They know you out here on the grind doin' ya thing, man. Elise says every time Ma sees you on TV, she stops everything."

CHAPTER 32

Summer 2001

TRUE TO HIS word, after the tour Danny took Trina and the kids to Disney World. They used Trina's mom's time share in Kissimmee, Florida, just west of Orlando on Lake Tohopekaliga. They were within driving distance of Disney World, Sea World, and Universal Studios.

Everyone wanted to go someplace different. Trina wanted to go to Sea World to see the dolphins. Danny and Jay wanted to ride the rides at Universal Studios, and Heaven wanted to see Minnie and all the other Disney characters.

"Well, it looks like there's only one thing to do here," Danny said, rubbing his hands together and standing in the middle of his family, while they stood silently waiting for the solution he would present. "Clearly we can't come to an agreement here so the only thing to do is just pack up and head back home right away."

"Daddy!" Little Heaven said, hitting him on the leg, knowing he was playing as Trina hit him on the arm at the same moment, saying he'd better stop playing.

"OK, so clearly this is a task for a fresh, bright, and more capable mind. Since my solution has been met with such violence and disdain, Jay, what do you propose we do at this juncture?" Danny said, attempting to sound intelligent and educated.

"What do I propose we do at this what-chure, Dad?" asked a confused Jay. Little Heaven looked on just as confused, standing beside her mom with her arms crossed, mimicking Trina as best she could.

"It's like saying 'at this place' or 'at this point in time' or 'where we find ourselves,'" Danny began to explain.

Trina cut in. "Simply put, baby, what do you think we should do now?"

"Well," Jay began, "since Heaven is the youngest who can say what she wants"—he smiled at his baby brother—"and both her and Junior would really like it if we went to Disney World, let's go there first. Then because Mommy wants to see the dolphins, we should go to Sea World next. This way, Mommy can be happy, and we can all go to Universal Studios where you and I want to go. And maybe Mommy will be so happy, she'll go on a ride with you and give you a big kiss!" he said, with it all figured out and unable to suppress his giggles.

"Spoken like a true team leader, a man of vision. I think we'll do just as you said, son, and see if Mommy gives me that big kiss." He shook hands with Jay, winking at Trina.

There were so many things to see and do at Disney World. Poor little Heaven tired herself out in no time at all and ended her day sleeping in her father's arms. Trina made a mental note to put her to bed a little earlier than usual, so she'd be more energized for all the extra fun and excitement.

By the time they headed home two weeks later, they'd visited Disney World a total of four times, Universal Studios five, and Sea World twice. By far, they had the most fun riding the rides at Universal Studios. There were games and game shows they participated in, and they even got to play around with the Nickelodeon characters.

Trina's mom and dad met them at Midway Airport in Chicago, where they dropped off the kids to them and hopped on a plane to Pine Bluff, Arkansas, to attend a surprise party for one of Danny's cousins. Later, they caught a flight to Cancun, where Stank and Joy met up with them for a vacation in paradise.

The couples landed at Cancun International Airport, where a limo was waiting to take them to the Grand Oasis Cancun. Twenty-five minutes later, the party of four stepped out of the limo and into the hotel's lobby, where they were greeted by dancers and frosty Cocos locos. The bellhops took their luggage up to their suites while they stayed in the lobby and enjoyed the welcome entertainment. The resort rested on almost a half mile of white sandy beach and was advertised as being the premier entertainment destination in Cancun. The available amenities were endless, from room service to wedding services to the twenty-four-hour doctor on call. They were shown to their luxurious suites and planned to reconvene an hour later after showering and allowing Joy to take a power nap.

The couples met back up an hour later and decided to head out for a bite to eat at a place call The Market Place. It was an international buffet-style restaurant that had been recommended by the concierge. There, they planned out the evening and activities for the following day, which would include waterskiing and parasailing for the fellas and sailing for the ladies. Later that night, they went to the Up and Down Disco and partied until it closed at 1:00 a.m. Then they walked along the shoreline barefoot on the sand, holding hands, gazing up at the stars, and looking out at the water.

The next morning, Danny and Stank met up and headed for the fitness center for an early morning workout before the girls were up and moving about. The center had the latest equipment—treadmills, row machines, ellipticals, and free weights. Danny had started working out a few months ago, so he knew his way around the gym. Stank was another story altogether. They had several laughs at his inability and lack of endurance to complete the workout sets Danny proposed, making for great memories of times shared.

They finished up with a twenty-minute run on the treadmill, where Stank nearly fell twice, and headed back to their suites to find notes from the girls saying to meet them over at a place called Joy's La Trattoria for an Italian breakfast. When they arrived, the girls had already ordered for them and decided the day's activities, both of which were surprises.

"I know y'all done lost ya damn minds now!" Danny said, stopping at the entrance of the nude beach area.

"Come on, baby. It'll be liberating and free," coaxed an enthused Trina.

"I ain't locked up, babe. I'm already liberated and free," Danny said resolutely.

"Don't look at me, brah. I promised to do whatever she wants on this vacation!" Stank submissively admitted, pulling his shirt over his head. "Thought you did too."

"Awe shit, brah, don't tell me you knew about this all along," Danny said with a betrayed defeated smirk, shaking his head.

Clearly, they wouldn't be waterskiing or parasailing today. He just shook his head as Stank shrugged his shoulders, surrendering to the tugging pull of Joy's hand as they walked away.

"Don't think you're getting off that easy. You owe me big-time for this one, Ms.!" Danny said, eyeing Trina while slipping out of his clothes.

"And Mama's gonna make it up to you, baby—*royally*, I promise!" She closed with a seductive peck on his lips.

Dinner was at Sarape, a Mexican restaurant where they tried different cultural dishes that were rumored to have aphrodisiacal effects, before heading over to the Ibiza Wet Bar for margaritas. There they drank and danced the night away. The guys weren't much for dancing but did all right by the ladies, just being able to follow the seductive rhythm of their hips. There was definitely some truth to the rumor about the Mexican food and its effects, as neither couple could contain the aggressive passion that coursed through them as they walked along the shores of the Caribbean Sea to their rooms.

Stank had to take Joy right then and there, and she had to be taken at that very moment; they kissed and fondled each other. They lay on the warm white sands totally naked, kissing. She mounted him and began riding slowly with a focused purpose. He responded in compliance to the tempered tempo of her hips as she glided in circular front to back motions.

"*Oooh, Daddy*!" she called breathlessly, overwhelmed by their synergy as she approached ecstasy. "Is it good to you, Daddy?" she whispered continuing her tyrannical stride.

He never knew pregnant pussy could be so damn good. He'd always felt Joy had some bomb pussy. But tonight, something had changed. Something was different that made it so much better somehow.

"Ahh, babe, this pussy is so good. You gonna make me co-co-come!" he said as he exploded deep inside her narrow, wet circumference.

Finally satisfied after having their full of love, they dressed and continued their stroll along the beautiful beach.

CHAPTER 33

Winter 2001

"BOY, IT'S COLDER than a hooker's heart out there. That wind blowing harder than a pissed-off pimp on a lazy hoe!" Jewabee said, stomping the snow off his feet as he stepped into the Harold's Chicken Shack.

"Gimme a half white fried hard with salt and pepper, a small order of gizzards, and put the mild sauce on the side in a cup foe me!" he barked, sliding a twenty-dollar bill through the money slot.

Fifteen minutes later, he walked out the door with his order and bumped into Tony on his way in. "Tony the muthafuckin' tiger. Nigga, I hear you doing *grrreat*! Nigga, shit'd!" he said animatedly like a pimp from the '70s.

Tony gave him some dap, and they embraced briefly. "What's good wit' it, Jew?"

"Man, if I had yo hands, I'd cut mines off; know what um sayin'? Nigga shit'd."

"You the man with the master plan, Jew. This yo world. I'm just a squirrel tryna get a nut, nigga, shit'd!" Tony said, mimicking the way Jewabee said 'nigga, shit'd' at the end of every sentence.

"True dat my nigga, true dat, nigga shit'd! But, yo, check dig. I'm sho

133

I got hoe that's ready to go, cuz every bitch in my stable is sho nuf able. Get at me, nigga, shit'd!"

All Tony could think about was the last time he'd messed with Jewabee and his so-called top-notch hoes. He could barely place his order because he and the girl behind the glass couldn't stop laughing at Jewabee after hearing him saying to someone he passed by on his way out the door, "Can a brotha of my complexion go in yo direction, Mz. thang—nigga, shit'd!

Tony finally got his order and was off to get his truck washed and detailed for his date with Loretta. This was their third date in two months, and the chemistry was definitely there. All that was needed was the right setting, and he knew he was getting the ass. For now, though, he would play the perfect gentlemen, pretending not to be hard-pressed for the drawers. He had a plenty of chicks on call waiting to bust down for him whenever he wanted, so he'd simply hit them up and be patient with Loretta.

"Hey, handsome!" Loretta greeted him as she came out of her building to an open card door held by him.

Giving him a quick peck on the lips, she entered the vehicle, and the night began. They were heading to see a Tyler Perry play at the Regal Theater on Stony Island and then to dinner at Ruth's Chris Steak House.

"Busy day at work today?" he asked, making small talk, and trying to engage her as he slipped in a Kem CD.

"Fridays are always busy days, you know—late court appearances, briefs and other filings are due, the meetings, you name it. Usually, I don't even get out of there before eight o'clock!"

"So, is it safe to say that I must be special for you to leave early tonight to be with me? And will you look at that, it's not even seven yet."

"Well, either that or I just really love Tyler Perry plays," she said with a smirk.

"Now that's cold. I'm crushed!" he said in a fake crestfallen tone.

"Awe, Antonio, poor baby," she replied, faking sympathy.

"Oh well, I guess I'll just have to get tickets to all of his shows—in every city he plays."

She looked over at him as he was saying this while shrugging his shoulders and just smiled. If felt good to have someone interested in her and what made her happy. She hadn't had that in forever. Her last boyfriend, Chester, if you could even call him that, had turned out to be a narcissistic jerk who sought to seize control of every aspect of her life, including her career. She knew Tony wasn't the plays or operas type, but the fact that he'd adjusted upon learning of her love for theater and taken the initiative to get tickets to shows and performances spoke volumes.

"Penny for your thoughts," he said, interrupting her fancy.

"I accept your offer, and I raise you five pennies for an honest answer and discussion on them."

Damn! she'd caught him off guard with that. "OK, shoot," he said.

"What do you want with me, Antonio? I mean clearly, we come from two different worlds. So, what are we doing here? Are we just having fun? I'm a big girl. You can give it to me straight!"

He thought for a moment before responding. "When I first saw you, I thought to myself that you'd be a nice fuck—to keep it 100! I mean, who wouldn't think that? Look at you; you're a beautiful, very sexy independent woman. What that says to me is that you know what you want and won't settle for less. Then after I started being around you, seeing you conduct business, I started to really see you—you know, who you are—and that made me want to know more of the you underneath the beauty and sexiness. Don't get me wrong, I still think you'd be a great fuck. But what I'm seeing makes me want to see more of you."

Now it was her turn to think, *damn*, as she let his response sink in. So, they rode without speaking for a while—nothing but Kem backgrounding their thoughts with warnings about when love calls your name.

Arriving at their destination, Tony parked in the lot across the street from the theater house. Shifting gears into park, he turned and asked, "Did I say something wrong in my answer to your question?"

She just sat there looking at him for a moment, and then without warning, she was over and on him, tongue kissing him and massaging his manhood.

After the play and dinner, they settled in at his place to finish what they'd begun earlier in the car. The Viagra pill he'd taken while at dinner kicked in, making his dick harder than Chinese arithmetic. The foreplay was brief. They kissed a little as he grabbed her ass, and she grabbed his penis then unfastened his belt. They were naked faster than Leslie Nielson in a sex scene in a comedy movie. This was no joke, though, as they made their way to the shower and got right down to business.

She was mesmerized by the size of his member. The girth made her mouth water as she got down on her knees and took in all that she could before the tip touched the back of her throat, and she moaned, relaxing her throat muscles and allowing further entrance. Tony's eyes rolled to the back of his head, and he caressed her scalp in the palms of his hands, slowly pumping in and out or her mouth.

Her head game is insane! he thought to himself and wanted to scream. He had never had his dick sucked like this. He unloaded and she gobbled up every bit like a bloodthirsty vampire extracting the life out of her victim.

Next, she climbed onto his bed on her hands and knees assuming the position like an obedient sex slave given the order, head down and ass pointed high to the sky at the bed's edge. He stepped up and slid into her like a Hall of Fame base runner sliding into home plate, feeling safe in heaven and engulfed by her paradise. He couldn't believe how tight and juicy her pussy was as he went in and out.

"Yeah, hit this pussy!" she demanded, throwing it back at him. "Fuck the shit outta me with' that big black dick."

Tony picked up the speed of his strokes. *This bitch is incredible!* he thought, slapping her on the ass and fucking her harder and harder.

He inserted his thumb into her asshole, sliding it in and out in sync with the concentrated strokes of his manhood and driving her crazy. She lay out flat, causing both his thumb and dick to ease out and rolled over onto her back, pulling her legs behind her head to reveal the prettiest pussy he had ever seen. He wasted no time digging in deep, like he was trying to reach her soul by way of her vagina.

"Ah shit, nigga, you all the way up in there. I feel it in my stomach. You, you tearing this pussy up!"

Seconds later, she cried out, "Oh, Jesus, I'm coming!"

Switching positions, she mounted him and began gyrating like she was on the dance floor, slow winding to a beat only she could hear—one that he could feel. It was like her pussy had fingers the way she massaged his dick. Within seconds, she had him hollering out in ecstasy, toes curled and shaking profusely.

Afterward, they lay there exhausted, staring at each other like two prizefighters after a twelve-round bout. Neither had expected the other to be so good in bed.

CHAPTER 34

"SPA DAY!" TRINA said to Joy and Tanya as the left North Riverside Mall. They had been Christmas shopping all morning and much of the afternoon. The G-Wagen was packed to capacity with bags.

"Girl, you read my mind, because my feet are killing me in these boots, and this damn baby got a sista's back feeling like it's about to break! But first I'm hungry and I gotta pee," Joy said from the back seat with bags all around and crowding her in. She was eight months pregnant with a due date of Christmas Day. "You two jingle bell heifers got me out here doing all this doggone walking!"

"Awe, sis-in-law, don't be such a scrooge! My little niece or nephew is gonna love all the pretty things we bought," Tanya said, looking back.

"You know what? I hope Rick gets your little happy ass pregnant with triplets! Then we'll see how you like having your body transformed and taken over by the little always hungry, always pissing creatures," Joy said, reclining her seat.

Trina and Tanya both laughed while Joy suppressed her laughter, pretending to be a little more upset than she really was. Trina laughed because, after having three kids, she knew exactly how Joy felt, while Tanya laughed because she was actually pregnant at that very moment. She and

Rick had decided they would keep it a secret until after Joy had her baby, though. That way, they wouldn't take the spotlight away from her and Stank. Tanya was a real sweetheart that way. She and Rick had recently gotten married, and she felt that it was her brother's turn to be the talk of their family. She was so happy that he'd left the streets alone and was in school doing something with his life. Her prayers had been answered.

The three women rode in silence, each lost in her own private thought. Joy thought of how badly she wanted to have sex and how the "No dick. It's too late in the pregnancy!" orders from her doctor made Stank's overprotective ass scared shitless to even touch her.

Trina's thoughts were of last night's lovemaking that had lasted till the early morning hours and had her still tingling, wanting more. Every time she thought about it, she got wet. Sex with Danny had always been the bomb. He knew her body, and it responded to his touch like that of no other man in the universe.

Tanya's thoughts were of the sex toys she'd slipped away to buy while Joy and Trina were in the Baby Gap going crazy. She couldn't wait to get home and try them out. This past month, she'd been so damn horny. Hell, she was hot and wet right now just thinking about what she planned to do to Rick tonight.

Trina was the first to abandon her thoughts, snatching the other women back to the here and now. "We're going to Sullivan's Steak House after that spa, girls. You can't eat now; it's gonna ruin your appetite," she added, looking through the review mirror at Joy for a brief second.

"Girl, as hungry as I am? Baby, bye! You betta pull this damn truck over there in that Wendy's before I jump out while we're still rolling. Damn Trina, girl, just let me pee at least—*and get me one of those singles and a fry and a frosty*," she said, mumbling the last part. "I'm still gonna be hungry, girl, I promise! This damn creature inside of me is never done feeding— *never*! Don't you see what it's doing to my body?"

Trina sighed as she pulled into the lot, sounding like a deflating beach ball.

After their spa treatments and dinner, Trina drove the girls back to her house. where they'd left their cars parked in her driveway, and the trio said their goodbyes.

All the lights were off when Trina entered through the front door.

"Don't turn on the lights, babe," Danny said from across the room as she felt for the switch.

"I got a big surprise for you, but first you have to find your way over to me without the aid of light."

Trina navigated her way over to where his voice was coming from through the darkness by memory and stood in front of his favorite recliner. Her hand touched his leg first, discovering he had no pants on. He ordered her not to touch him immediately, and to just stand there. She did just as he instructed. Next, he stood and began undressing her, starting with her hat, coat, and scarf. After discarding those items, he bent and kissed her ever so softly with passion that made her clitoris pound and throb in her thong.

She tried to help undress herself, but he stopped her. Taking his time unbuttoning her blouse, he began nibbling on her right earlobe and kissing her hot spot right beneath her ear along her neckline, driving her wild. He unfastened her bra, freeing her perfect breasts and greeted them each with the little sucking kisses she loved so much while unzipping her pants.

After she was completely naked, he retook his seat and ordered her to climb aboard. As she began climbing on top of him, he cuffed her at the back of her knees and lifted her until he was face-to-face with her womanhood.

"Oooh, baby, yeah. Eat this pussy. Ohhh, bae!" she stammered as he feasted hungrily on her juicy fruit. She did all she could to hang on to her sanity as he nibbled on her pulsating clit, licking and blowing gently at intervals, causing her legs to shake and tremble uncontrollably, where they rested around his neck.

"Oooh, oooh, I'm coming bae. Shi-ahh-it!" she cried as she released her cream filling so desperately sought by him. "Ooh, baby, you gotta put it in!" she moaned.

Danny released his grip, allowing her to slide down his chest where she landed perfectly on his palpitating member, filling her love canal with total satisfaction. Grabbing her ass cheeks in each hand, he squeezed gently, pulling them up and apart as he lifted her up to the tip of his dick and then down to meet its base as he rolled his hips, thrusting deep inside her.

"This pussy is so good, babe! Whose pussy is this?" he said breathlessly in between strokes.

"This yo pussy, Daddy! This Danny's pussy, every inch of it!" she answered.

"Well then, turn around and ride this dick backward and show Daddy how you work them pussy muscles!"

Without delay she stood, turned around and straddled him once again, sliding down his magic pole of pleasure like an experienced firefighter over, and over again. The way she rode him backward always drove him insane. She would clench her pussy muscles as she rose to his tip and then releasing them as she slid down again. It was paralyzing to him, putting him at her mercy with every stroke.

Feeling the slight jerks from him that were so familiar, she knew he was approaching his climax. She paused at the base with him all the way inside of her and worked her muscles, contracting them and releasing them slowly for about twenty seconds. Then just when his approach seemed to subside, she clenched her pussy muscles as tight as she could and rose to the tip of his dick once more before winded back down, causing him to erupt violently inside of her.

Regaining his composure, he matched her rhythmic twirls with short deep strokes while passionately massaging one of her breasts as she seductively sucked the other. It was now his turn to take control and punish her mercilessly with pleasure. He stood without extracting himself from inside her and bent her over the coffee table and continued his pounding assault, plunging deep inside her. He took his time, giving her the long deep strokes, her body craved, driving her mad.

"Oooh, right there, bae. Ahh, ahh, ooh dig this pussy out, baby. You fuckin' the shit outta me, Big Daddy!" she exclaimed.

Afterward, all she could do was stare after him as he moved through the darkness toward their bedroom. She got up and followed him as if gravitational pull was dragging her. She wanted to remain close to him. She needed to; his love was her oxygen, and she needed to breathe. Her only desire at that moment was to bring him joy and pleasure as she placed her warm mouth around his now semihard tool of reckoning and began performing her inherent duty.

CHAPTER 35

"THERE'S THE HEAD. OK, Joy, give me one more push. Give me a good hard one this time!" the doctor coached.

Joy had been in labor for seven hours. After her water broke, nothing could describe the immense pain she felt with each contraction. Her sister-in-law, Tanya, had advised her to take the epidural shot to ease the pain, but she'd refused, insisting on having a natural birth.

"Joy, babe, we can do this!" Stank said encouragingly.

Stank had been there for the past five and half hours, Kneeling at her bedside and holding her hand. Every time another contraction came, she became increasingly irritated with him. Even the sound of his voice saying, "*We* can do this, Joy." made her want to just slap him.

"You did this to me! So just shut your face!" she said, sounding like the girl from the movie *The Exorcist*.

Stank kept silent after that, eyes bulging and sweat trickling down the sides of his face like he was the one having the baby.

"Good push, Joy!" the doctor said just before the beautiful screams of their baby girl filled the room.

"It's a girl," the nurse announced excitedly.

Joy lay there, tears streaming down her face, feeling what only a mother can feel after bringing forth life as the nurse handed her beautiful baby girl to her wrapped in a pink blanket.

"She's gorgeous!" was all Stank could manage before choking up.

"Janeasha," Joy said, gently stroking her baby's silky hair that stuck out from underneath the little cap the nurse had placed on her head.

Joy's mom and Stank's aunt Brenda were at the house waiting for the new parents to arrive with the newest edition to their families. A banner was stretched across the front of the house that read, "It's a Girl!" in pink letters. Balloons were tied to the rails, streaming happily in the wind—some pink and some yellow.

The two aunties raced out the door to meet them as they pulled into the driveway like siblings competing to ride shotgun.

All Stank could do was help Joy into the house, as the baby nappers had already snatched up his little sleeping beauty and whisked her away. Rick and Tanya showed up to meet the new one, followed by Danny and Trina an hour later. The men went down into Stank's man cave, leaving the women alone with his sleeping princess. They drank and shot pool, half watching the game on TV.

"What's up, what's up, what's up! You know I had to come and check out the little one," Tony said as he made his way down the basement stairs, carrying a fifth of Rémy XO and cigars.

"No doubt, my nigga, no doubt!" Stank said as they embraced.

"Tee, what's good, brah!" Danny asked as they dapped and hugged.

"I'm tryna figure out how this ugly-ass dude made such a beautiful baby!"

"You know what they say, the ugliest muthafuckas make the prettiest babies," Stank said, shrugging his shoulders.

"I don't know, brah. You sho that's yo baby up there?" Tony said, laughing as Stank gave him a playful shove.

"Rick!" Tony said as they clasped hands and shoulder hugged. "Man, every developer in the city and county has your name on their lips! Don't forget the little people when you get to the top." Tony gave him a chummy elbow to the ribs.

It was true; Cordelle Architecture Designs was the firm everybody wanted on their construction projects. Attorney Kline had really given Rick's career a boost with all the business she'd ushered his way.

"It's all God, brah man; it's all Him," Rick responded modestly.

"I hear you're having a grand opening for your new club Naked' on New Year's Eve," Rick added, shifting the attention back to Tony. "That's all I've been hearing on the radio lately. Sounds like it's gonna be like that!"

"Yeah, me and my boy Troy went in together on that. We 'bout ta make it pop off!"

"Troy off Washington and 29th Street?" Rick inquired, taking a swallow from his beer.

"Yeah, his moms stay over that way. You know him?" Tony responded, cuing his pool stick.

"Yeah, I know Troy. We used to run together when we were kids back in grammar school—me him, Phil, and Bang. Bang and Phil got killed here not too long ago for some stickup mess they were into, I hear. We used to be thick as thieves as kids. I stopped hanging with them fools right after eighth grade pretty much; my mom's wasn't having it at all! I went away to college, and they went their way. They tried to jump me once when I was home on break for the holidays, and I haven't messed with them since," Rick said, taking the last swallow of his beer.

Tony and the others stood listening to Rick, all the while communicating with one another with their eyes in the shadows of Rick's vision.

"It's going down, baby boy. I got reservations for all y'all and ya ladies in VIP!" Tony said, changing the subject, playing it off. "Oh shit, Stank. You might not be able to make it with the new baby and all," he said on second thought.

"Yeah, I may have to sit this one out, brah, you know, and bring it in with my two leading ladies here at the house."

"I gotta get going, y'all. Early day tomorrow. Closing out the books for the last quarter of the year. But you can be sure that me and the Mrs. will be there New Year's Eve," Rick said with a stretch and yawn before heading upstairs to retrieve his new bride.

Rick's revelation had blown Tony's mind, but he was careful not to allow his body language to show it in Rick's presence. He had been hanging out with Troy like they were brothers for the past year, when all along he was the enemy.

"Aye, brah, you already know what's gotta happen. You know what you gotta do," Danny said, looking Tony in the eyes. "If this nigga got the balls to come at you like that and then be under you like nothin's happened, either he's a damn fool or he's playin' you for one. Either way, it's a danger to us all, brah!" he continued.

"Yeah, you're right if he—" Tony began.

But Danny cut him off. "If he? Come on, Tee man. You just heard the man say he knew him, and that's the type of shit he was known for. He stood right here and told you that he ran with both of them other niggas and that they got murked over some stickup shit! How much plainer do you need shit to be? That nigga was in on that shit, brah. He was the link to you, cuz you ain't even know them clown-ass niggas. Now this pussy-ass nigga all up in ya face like you ain't gone do shit! Only question here is whether you're gonna do what needs to be done, or do we have to?" Danny said, glancing over at Stank.

"Naw, my nigga, I got this. Y'all my brothers, and I love ya!" Tony said, sitting on one of the bar stools. "I gotta tell y'all something, and I don't know how y'all gone see me afterwards. But I gotta put it out there to you and let the chips fall where they may. Them people jumped down on me last summer not too long after I saw you at the wedding. They wanted me to set you up, but I wouldn't do it. I couldn't do it, brah! I knew you had already shaken loose from the game. So, I agreed to do it just to get a bond.

"After I was out for a few weeks, I told them that you must have found out that I was working with them because you weren't taking any of my calls anymore. When they saw I wouldn't help get you, they started with the life in prison threats again. At that point, I was ready to run. I was gonna go to Colombia and stay away from the States.

"Then this new special agent chick shows up outta nowhere with a hard-on for my brother-in-law, Edwardo. I gotta tell you right or wrong that I said fuck him cuz I ain't neva liked his bitch ass anyway. So ah, that's what it is and why I ain't been around y'all. I wanted to tell y'all when I saw y'all down in South Carolina, but figured it wasn't the right time. So that's the whole of it right there. I could never do you, brah, neither of you niggas. I love y'all. Y'all my brothers!" Tony confessed.

Danny was noticeably stunned at the news of the Feds interest in him to say the least, but the fact that Tony had ever agreed to work with them was unsettling—even if it was just to get a bond as he said. He no longer felt Tony could be trusted, and his mind was racing in reverse, trying to remember all he'd disclosed with Tony over the past couple of years.

He knew he could easily account for his lifestyle and al that he had. He'd received $175,000 when he was nineteen years old from the accident he was in, and his mom had made several investments in real estate, mutual funds, and municipal bonds. During his last few years in the game, he'd lived modestly, not dressing flashy or spending money flamboyantly.

Still, he knew the Feds didn't operate on truth and real evidence. They built cases on lies to further their cause, whatever that was at the time.

CHAPTER 36

AFTER LEARNING OF Troy's involvement in the robbery, Tony drove out to Loretta's house in Brookfield to plan his next move. He and Loretta had been dating strong for a little while now. He felt like he could ease his mind a bit with his dick down her throat, and then afterwards he'd be able to think more clearly. Everything revolved around a nut for him, and this was no different.

He rubbed the scar over his left eye, thinking of the night he had been kidnapped. Suddenly, a light bulb popped on in his mind, illuminating that once dark place that held the detailed events of that night. *There was a third man!* He could now see it clearly. He remembered the exchange of gunfire and the running toward the garage through the kitchen when another masked figured stepped out and shot him point-blank. "Son of a bitch," he muttered, gripping the steering wheel tighter and simultaneously pressing the gas pedal.

He'd finally lined up the dots. Troy had to have been there, one of the masked men. His mind raced through different scenarios of how and why he should have known, like red lights in a high-speed chase arriving at just one dictum: "You know what's gotta happen!"

———————⟫⟪———————

For the next few days, Tony carried on as if nothing was wrong. He and Troy got things in order for the grand opening and hung out like always. The only thing different was Tony's cautious eye on Troy and the snub-nosed .38 he now carried in the small of his back. He'd called in a little muscle from Miami, disguised as cousins on his mother's side just in town to bring in the new year.

Although Tony seemed a little distant at times, Troy just shrugged it off attributing it to the unannounced guests. They all hung out at the doghouse for the first couple of nights smoking and drinking with a few chicks Tony called on to kick it.

Only Tony knew of the demise he had planned for Troy, not even the so-called muscle. The details of the job were kept from them because, after much thought, Tony concluded that, to carry out his plan, he needed Troy to remain completely relaxed and unsuspecting. If Troy suspected even the slightest thing was amiss, he would surround himself with his men. That would be no good, as it would mean more bodies. And with more bodies, there was always a greater chance for things to go sideways. Troy was no dummy, and Tony knew this. He also knew that Troy was a man of war, the way the way he was not. But where Troy outmuscled him, he'd outthink Troy. And ultimately it would come down to who thought the best and nothing else, he reasoned.

———————⟫⟪———————

The night before New Year's Eve, Troy was taking Tony's cousins to get some jerk chicken over on Cottage Grove as a favor to Tony while he went to take care of some business. He was in the process of telling them about the city when, out of nowhere, the one in the back seat put a gun to his head and told him to pull the car over on the next block. Immediately, Troy's mind went into survival mode as he did what he was told. Before he could get the car fully in park, he felt a sharp blow to the side of his head, and everything went black.

Swack! Troy woke up to Tony standing in front of him. He didn't know how long he'd been unconscious or how many time he'd been out. His vision was blurred by the blood cascading from somewhere above his eyes. He knew he'd been tortured, but to what extent was impossible to know due to the numbness and his inability to see clearly.

"*Bitch-ass nigga*! You rob me and try to kill me and then have the nerves to come around like I wouldn't find out? Like nothing would happen to yo ass?" Tony now spoke with a thicker accent.

Thwack! He was out again.

<hr/>

When Troy came to, Tony was nowhere to be seen, and only one of the cousins remained close by to keep watch over him.

"Hey, Chio!" Troy called out to him.

Chio only looked but didn't respond.

"I gotta piss, man. Let me go piss," Troy said trying to figure out his escape.

But this time, Chio didn't even look his way, like he could no longer hear English. Troy sat there trying to engage him in conversation as he worked to free his hands, but Chio refused to acknowledge him or even look his way—*big mistake*.

A little later, Tony and the other cousin, called Omar, returned. They wheeled in a cart with what appeared, from where Troy sat, to be a truck battery, jumper cables, and a bucket of water.

"Ahhh, sssshhhhhit!" Troy said feeling the sting of the liquid contents from the bucket he now knew to be saltwater as Tony squeezed it over his head and it ran down over the open wounds. Troy tried to remain calm so as not to reveal that his hands were free.

Next, Tony connected one end of the cables to the battery. Then, as he attempted to put the other end on Troy, Troy leaped up backward over the chair, at the same time, thrusting the chair forward into Tony's path of motion. Out of pure reflex, Tony attempted to stop the chair coming his way and to keep himself from falling over it because of the forward momentum he'd built up. When the cables contacted the metal chair, he received the shock meant for Troy, sending him to the ground momentarily paralyzed. The abrupt chaos threw the other two mentally off balance—just long enough for Troy to siege the gun Chio had once guarded him with and fire once, hitting Omar center of mass in the chest and knocking him to the ground, before diving out the window.

Troy ran as fast as his legs would allow him to in the cold before stumbling to the ground in the Walgreen's parking lot at 87th and Cottage Grove, where an old woman saw him and dialed 9-1-1. The paramedics arrived and took him to the local hospital, where they treated and released him after he had no statement for the police.

Exhaustion kept him hidden away for the first two days, embarrassment for the next few, while he licked his wounds and plotted. He'd pretty much kicked the coke habit over the past year, but right now, he needed it to make the pain go away. The number of cuts to his body were too many to count. He felt like he'd been skinned, there were so many cuts and slashes. His nose was broken, and both his eyes were bloodshot with dark purple rings underneath them.

His pride wouldn't allow him to be seen like this. So for now, killing Tony would have to wait. In the meantime, he would have to heal and plan his attack.

Winters in Chicago were cold to say the least, but January was one of the coldest, if not the coldest, months. Blistering winds ripped through with disrespectful violations of the worst kind, causing those who unfortunately had to venture into the outdoors for even the briefest periods to cover their faces and step lively.

Tonight, Troy would stick his head out from his hole to see what was going on in the city—***his city***! It had been just over a week since the incident, and he had healed just enough to resurface. He went, riding the lonely, deserted streets in an old Ford Bronco, like a hungry lion roaming the jungle.

CHAPTER 37

YOU COULD HAVE bought Loretta for a nickel if you'd told her she'd be not only involved with a street dude but also pregnant by him at thirty-nine years old. Sure, the sex was good, great in fact, explosive even. She was older than him, his senior by more than five years, approaching her prime with a sex drive that only a younger man could handle. There was just something about the rough edges of a thug that turned her on to no end. It had always been that way for her for as long as she could remember.

In high school, it had been John Robert, always fighting and getting into trouble, who'd made her skip class to ride on his motorbike. It had nearly given her father an aneurysm. "Bad association spoils useful happiness!" he used to say. Or her favorite was, "If you lie down with dogs, you'll get up with flees!" Then there had been George, aka Georgie Porgie, DePaul's star point guard, who was arrested for running a drug ring on campus. What could she say? She liked bad boys.

She knew her father would never approve of Tony, not the three-time senator of the Sunshine State, Mr. Subcommittee Chairman himself. Not a snowball's chance in hell! For her entire life, she'd been walking on eggshells around her father, scared to be who she was, too afraid Daddy wouldn't be proud of her if she didn't do this or didn't like doing that. So, she'd willed herself not to like street dudes because they were bad boys and Daddy didn't approve of bad boys. Instead, she'd dated the supposedly good boys, who'd walked all over her heart and couldn't fuck their way out of a paper bag.

So, for the last seven years, she'd been doing her—fucking bad boys and satisfying her sexual appetite. *To hell with what Daddy doesn't like or approve of. He's getting his rocks off, so why shouldn't I?* was her reasoning.

Tony was something different though. He was the nut that cut! Not only had she let him fuck her without protection, she'd let herself fall for him.

"Ms. Kline!" Her gynecologist called her name for the fourth time, snatching her from her deep thoughts.

"I'm sorry. What did you say, Dr. Coleman?"

"When do you want to schedule your prenatal care?"

"Oh, um, sure," was all she could manage still not fully hearing or understanding what was being said. She was too taken back by the news of her pregnancy to give a competent answer to any question—not even what her name was.

CHAPTER 38

"FUCK, FUCK, FUCK!" Tony said, kicking the chair beside him as he sat nervously, pondering how to tell Edwardo that Omar had been killed. To make matters worse, he had never even gotten the OK to bring Omar and his brother Chio to Chicago for the bullshit he was on. He knew he should've just simply put a bullet in Troy's head. But no, he had to play big shit hard to flush, and now Omar was dead.

Tony couldn't explain the reasoning behind his actions to save his life. And after the conversation with Elise, he knew it may come down to just that, his reasoning. However, telling Edwardo was no longer necessary, because not only had he been told, but he was also already in route to the states according to Elise.

"That fucking Chio!" he muttered, frustrated by the news. He'd told him not to say anything. Hell, he'd practically begged him. "But nooo, this little shit just had to go and open his fuckin; mouth!" he thought aloud.

He could lose his life behind this. Edwardo was not a man to be crossed in any way, shape, or form. And he was already helping the fed build a criminal case against him.

Gotta save my ass for now. I'll worry about my face later, he told himself. But truth be told, it wasn't his face that would be in danger; it was his very life. He'd seen what happened to those who were disloyal to or who stole from the cartel, and the results were always the same, death. How much worse would it be for him when he wasn't even a member of the cartel, and it was his fault Omar lay in the Cook County Morgue? Not to mention Edwardo would be going to jail for the rest of his life because of him.

The Dominguez Cartel was not a band of vandals raping and pillaging all in their path; they were not the best of their countrymen but certainly not the worst. They did not extort small business owners working hard to make an honest living. Nor did they abduct and enslave young women to work their fields and satisfy their sexual desires. They produced and sold drugs, period. If you got in the way of that or brought harm to La Familia, you found yourself in grave danger.

Edwardo Comez was Tony's brother-in-law, and he was a very powerful man who some would even describe as a malignant narcissist. He was El Capo of the Dominguez Cartel. And unfortunately for Tony, Omar was his favorite little cousin. Tony wasn't in the Dominguez Cartel, but he was considered La Familia because he was Elise's brother. And for that reason, he was permitted to receive as many kilo a month as he could handle—that and the fact that Elise had convinced Edwardo to allow him to conduct business in Chicago.

Edwardo wanted no personal interests in the northern states for the cartel. He felt the distance the drugs had to travel to reach their destinations could be problematic. He did, however, welcome the business of those in the North willing to make the trip down to Florida to purchase their product. But there would be no consignment agreements with them. Edwardo didn't want the risk associated with shipping there. And with 80 percent control of the cocaine trade in the east, he didn't need to.

Tony was a nervous wreck, even to the point of shaking uncontrollably. His teeth chattered, and the sudden chill he felt caused sporadic Tourette's syndrome-like jerks. He'd just been told of Edwardo's arrival in Chicago and that he'd been summoned.

He arrived at the Palmer House hotel with bubbles in his gut and his heart in his throat. Chio was in the lobby waiting to bring him to Edwardo's suite without delay. If looks could kill, Chio would be dead a thousand times over the way Tony stared at the back of his head on the ride up to the 23rd floor in the elevator.

Chio tapped on the door a few times, and it opened. An enormous, crater-faced Colombian with a thick goatee and a long ponytail stood before them. He stepped aside, permitting them entrance before patting Tony down. Tony knew the pat down was routine; every time he'd met with Edwardo, this had occurred. But even so, he felt the need to speak of the lack of its necessity.

"I would never disrespect you and bring—" he began.

"But you already have, Antonio," Edwardo said as he raised a hand, silencing Tony instantly from where he sat on the sofa drinking a glass of iced tea.

"And because of this disrespect, Omar is dead, and we find ourselves here."

Crater Face stepped up behind Tony like a bailiff in a courtroom proceeding preparing to take him into custody. Fear flooded Tony like raw sewage into a basement during a terrible rainstorm. His knees went weak as his mind replayed the gruesome things, he'd seen his brother-in-law do to others who'd crossed him in the past. Suddenly, the thought of Edwardo having knowledge of his dealings with the Feds invaded his mind and paralyzed him to the point he began stuttering.

"Edwa-wa-wado, it it it was ne-never my intention to dis-dis-disrespect you. I-I-I never meant for Omar to be ki-killed. This was one-one of the men who robbed me fo-for your mo-money and tried to ki-kill me. When I le-learned of this I wanted revenge, and-and nothing else. It wa-was stu-stupid of me to bring Chio and O-O-Omar here. It is my fault he is dead."

"I understand revenge, Antonio, and I do not blame you for wanting to kill this guy. Because this is the man that has stolen from La Familia and tried to take away your life, I will forgive you for your part in Omar's death. But this man must pay with his life."

The Colombians stormed the city like ants to a picnic. Though the Bros were one of the more structured gangs of the city, they were no match for the Dominguez Cartel. They killed so many of the Bros that the city's crime rate dropped noticeably by 30 percent almost overnight. There were few shoot-outs in the streets and even fewer bodies lying in the gutters than was the norm in war, just disappearances. The construction site where the strip mall was to be erected held so many of the Bros dead corpses it was like their very own private cemetery.

The cartel continuously combed the neighborhoods searching for Troy, but he was nowhere to be found. Tony led the charge, transformed by the horrendous acts he'd witnessed and even participated in in the past few weeks. He was not the same man. His thoughts had become more sinister and eviler, his actions more calculated. He would no longer chase Troy. He would make Troy come to him.

CHAPTER 39

HE LAY BLINDFOLDED on his back, arms stretched wide. Both wrists were handcuffed to the cast-iron headboard, both ankles cuffed in the same fashion at the other end. He was helpless, just the way he liked it, as she rode him mercilessly like an experienced bull rider atop a mechanical bull in slow motion, chanting, "Oooh, Daddy!" seductively, just the way he liked it.

His wife would never—could never—satisfy his sexual appetite the way this enchantress woman did. Although he couldn't see her face for the mask she wore during their sessions, her mesmeric eyes captivated him as her sweet, childlike voice allured him to a pit of helpless ecstasy, where the gyration of her hips took over and subdued him under her rune. Besides, he didn't care what her facial expressions were. He only saw heaven when she rode him, chanting, "Ooh, Daddy!"

She was a sex goddess. He never knew what to expect with her. She had many tricks in her depository of treats. She made him feel alive. He felt happiness and joy inside of her.

His marriage had become a deathly boring routine he was sure was slowly killing him. The marital felicity was long gone for what seemed like light-years. His wife treated him like sex was dirty and his fantasies of being dominated were somehow sadistic and immoral. He wanted out! He wanted freedom from the monotonous performance he was forced to yield day in and day out to her. He wanted her to go away and for his sex goddess to take her place.

Divorce was not an option. Surely, he would walk away with nothing but humiliation. The last twenty-two years of blood, sweat, and tears he'd put into the company—her father's company and … her company—would all be flushed down the drain. Her mother and brother sat on the board of directors. They'd find reason to kick him out into the cold for sure, blaming him for the dissolvement of the marriage. Her mom, the old whatever filthy name that came to mind whenever he thought of her, had never liked him to begin with. It was her father who had recognized his business acumen and ability to lead Raybon Developments into the twenty-first century—so much so that he'd passed over his own son and chosen him to be his successor. No, divorce most certainly was not an option.

Pretty rode on, holding on to the leather leash clamped to the collar around his neck like a lonely cowboy on a tired, run-down horse along a lonely trail. It was all a job to her—no fun, no pleasure, just work. Most of what he requested repulsed her to no end. Any man wanting to be fucked in the ass, dildo, or dick, was gay in her eyes, plain and simple. *Rich sick, SOB!* she thought as she gripped the leash tighter and rode faster causing him to scream out like a little bitch begging for mercy.

At the end of their session, she uncuffed him and began dressing. He sat up, his back resting against the headboard that had arrested his mobility only moments ago, watching her in a trancelike state.

"What?" She looked back at him as she buttoned her blouse, no longer wearing the mask.

"I could take you away from all of this. You know what I'm saying? I could rescue you," he said in an urgent hushed tone.

"Who said I needed someone to rescue me? Look, go on home to your wifey, sweetie—to that big house in the hills I know you got," she said slipping into her jeans.

"What if I don't want her? What if I want you?" he asked, his tone more earnest now.

"And what's wifey gonna do, just pack up and go away quietly so we can live happily ever after?" she said, pretending to entertain the thought as she moved about getting dressed to leave.

"There could be an accident or something. You know, accidents do happen all the time," he responded, enthusiasm dripping from his voice.

"Go on home to the wife, Johnny. This isn't what you want; trust me," she said, walking out the door. *He's ready for the pickin'; that much is for sure*, Pretty thought to herself, removing his Black Card from her bra as she pulled away from the parking garage, dialing Sharon's number.

"Gimme a call when you get this, gurl," Pretty said, leaving a voice message.

<hr>

"And gurl, this nicca got to talkin' 'bout how he could save me and how he don't want his wife no more and she could have an accident and shit." Pretty went on telling Jenny and Sharon about her morning with Johnny. They knew of John's strange sexual fantasies. They'd each experienced his insistent sexual impulses, both individually and together. He was a freak to say the least, but he was a target all the same. And his pockets were ripe for the picking.

"Is he stupid?" Jenny cut in.

"Gurl, after I cuffed that damn card, I was in exit mode. I played the role like an A-list actress right on out the doe. 'And Wifey's just gonna pack up and go away quietly so we can live happily ever after?'" Pretty said before taking a bow.

And they all high-fived, laughing.

"And the Oscar for best performing actress in *Trick Dat Nigga If You Can* goes to …" Jenny joked.

"What's so funny, y'all?" Aleithia walked in.

"Oh, nothing really. Pretty was just telling us how she was thinking of conspiring to commit murder," Jenny said, sitting cross-legged on the kitchen counter.

"Murder? Bitch, I know you playing'!" Aleithia said, directing deadpan eyes toward Pretty.

"Don't listen to her. That hoe is crazy!" Pretty said and began retelling the story of her morning with Johnny.

"That nicca's a creep to the tenth power! Ain't he the same nicca that wanted you to piss in his face, Jenny?" Aliethia asked.

"Mmmhumph!" She nodded, eating a spoonful of Nutella with the spoon upside down sticking out of her mouth.

"Alrighty then, let me see. Gonna go to PayPal. Okey dokey." She spoke more to herself than to anyone else. "Let's see how much Mr. Bradford wants to donate to the Kute Kittens Charity."

Kute Kittens Charity was just one of many for-profit organizations Tamera had created to transfer the stolen funds. There, the funds would sit for the required seventy-two-hour waiting period before being transferred to one of their other shell companies and then to their offshore accounts in the Cayman Islands. By the time the monies arrived at their offshore accounts, so many transactions had taken place, there was no way of tracing it.

"OK, $723,586.42," she continued as if speaking to the screen. "Last large purchase was for $219,000 and change. Ladies, I think the freaky Mr. Bradford wants to donate $175,000 to the Kute Kittens Charity because he just loves pussy cats. And on behalf of kute kittens everywhere, I accept this generous contribution with a grateful *meeow*," she finished as she pressed enter, completing the transaction.

Now seeing it in action, Pretty understood the need for the equipment. The scrambler software was a simple chip that allowed someone to move through cyberspace without leaving a footprint. It made determining the IP address used in a transaction impossible because it literally sent dozens of IP addresses everywhere at once and then again after thirty seconds or however long the person using it chose. It burned the footprints, leaving no trace of the transaction.

Pretty nodded with a satisfied smile, happy she'd listened to Sharon and Jenny. At first, she had been reluctant to fork over so much money for something she hadn't ever heard of and didn't understand. But after handing down grave warnings of death for betrayal and considering the possibility of them all spending forever in jail if they got caught because they didn't have it, she'd agreed.

The scrambler software was the most expensive and hardest to obtain of all the equipment according to Sharon, as you couldn't just run out and buy it from your local Radio Shack. This was truly high-tech equipment used by foreign governments and terrorists. Sharon could download the software from the chip onto fire sticks, enabling them to use it on any computer anywhere, which added mobility to their operation. Yes, this was certainly high-tech, and you had to have connections to get it— connections in places like Russia or somewhere over in the Middle East.

If the troubles of yesterday could ever be considered preparations for today's opportunities that brought about the successes of tomorrow, no greater witness could be found than Jenny's wasted chance to study abroad in Russia through the exchange student program. She'd been caught in bed with the son of the host by the host herself, who was convinced that Jenny was nothing more than a promiscuous girl who'd taken advantage of her baby. Her son, Ira, was no baby though, at least not according to Jenny. In fact, she was giving him the gift of love for his approaching eighteenth birthday just days before they were caught. Consequently, Jenny had been terminated from the program for that year at the complaint of the host and sent back to the States.

For a while, she and Ira had continued to communicate via Facebook until things had fizzled out. Last she'd heard from him; he was applying for the exchange student program here in the States. Just the thought of Ira made her moist. To this day, he was sexiest computer geek she'd ever been with—not that she'd ever been with any other computer geeks. But he was that dude, she confessed as she scrolled through his Facebook page.

After a few inboxes and phone calls, she'd hopped a plane with Sharon and Pretty to Boston, Massachusetts, from where the four of them had flown over to Moscow and purchased the software.

Next up was Tamera, a business administration major who understood both business principles and practices, including accounting. She created the shell corporations and for-profit charities. Together with Sharon and Jenny, the three funneled the money they stole through these phony entities before disbursing them to the offshore accounts they held in the Cayman Islands. They each received a salaried amount of $2,500 bimonthly from Dime-A-Dozen, one of the shell corporations disguised as a consultant firm doing consultations for all the for-profit charities they held, like Kute Kittens. Yes, Pretty had struck gold with the commencement of the Pussy Kat Klique, she thought as Jenny hit the enter key and the screen read, "Transaction complete."

"Meeow," she returned.

Like taking candy from a baby, Pretty thought to herself as she looked down upon the City of Angels from one of the floor-to-ceiling windows of their condo forty stories above. They were only blocks away from the Ritz Carton, the STAPLES Center, and LA Escape. Most game nights, they could be found at special after-game parties for certain players.

BC had yet to resurface, but there were rumors he was playing overseas. Pretty continued to avoid the cameras and media attention surrounding the fanfare of the ballplayers and stars she encountered and often accompanied. She would, for now, remain dead and buried to those from her past life in Chicago, over 2,400 miles away.

CHAPTER 40

January 2002

THE WAR WITH Tony seemed to escalate by the second, with each attack like a tennis match between Venus and Serena. Tony's "cockroach band," as Troy referred to them, were kidnapping the Bros in broad daylight, right off the streets where they hung and hustled. Troy and his main five men rode day and night on the hunt for Tony and anyone who resembled a Colombian or was even of Spanish descent.

It wasn't even February yet, and the city of Chicago was already set to be the murder capital of the nation, with sixty-three murders less than a month into the new year. This didn't even account for the dozen or so Bros buried at the construction site where Tony had broken ground to build the strip mall in Chatham.

Missing person reports were growing. But because it was basically drug-dealing gangbangers among the missing, the police turned a deaf ear to the outcry of the community. Edwardo Comez and the Dominguez Cartel were a storm The City That Works was not prepared to deal with. As ironic as it sounds, the boldness of the attacks launched by the cartel was more than likely the reason they appeared to go unnoticed. Their guerilla warfare tactics didn't allow them to be concerned with the police enough to fear them in the least bit. They were above the local authorities in their homeland and had little regard for their lives, or any human life for that matter. Troy had never encountered a war of this magnitude. He'd never faced an enemy so fierce. He was used to being the madman on the loose who all were wary of because he was so unpredictable. Now the unknown Colombian was the crazy man running wild. And Troy knew it was only a matter of time before they met in the center to dance.

Troy watched the transactions his young foot soldiers conducted as they ran back and forth to the approaching customers. The hood was the safest place, where everything was familiar and anyone or anything out of place would be noticed immediately.

"On that car! On that car!" one of the youngsters shouted from the opposite end of the block, causing everyone to take notice of the old brown Buick as it slowly made its way up the block.

Guns were drawn and at the ready by hooded figures emerging from the shadows of gangways as if out of thin air. Two industrial-sized dumpsters were rolled out into the middle of the street at the end of the block forbidding passage. Once everyone was satisfied it was just a Mexican family of four, a mother, father, and two small children, they were allowed safe transit.

Troy settled back into his state of observation in the black Econovan parked in the middle of the block. He wanted to be in the center of the action should anything happen. The AK-47 lay at his side between him and his most trusted solider, Paco, while his favorite twin Carbine-15s lay at the ready across both their laps. The remaining four of his main five men were strategically placed. Two were in the attics of houses on either side of where he sat parked, watching out of windows. The other two were watching his mother's house a block over. The home invasion and pistol whipping they'd given Tony's father was sure to be responded to with a visit to Troy's mother's residence, he suspected.

As the sun set, the snow began its descent from the heavens to the earth like tiny pieces of confetti covering everything below. Troy sat lost in thought, watching but not seeing much outside the van. *How did it come to this?* was the question painted on the blackboard of his mind. His life's events played across the screen of his mind like an old 35 mm film. If it wasn't one thing, it was always another, he thought. The decisions he'd made in the past had always been predicated upon who he was trying to be or who he thought he had to be. He was trapped inside the madness of poor choices that brought a never-ending stream of trouble. This whole war with Tony was Phil's fault. He's told Phil and Bang they didn't need to rob Tony. Now he was at war with the Colombians by himself, and Phil was nowhere in sight, as if he'd escaped through death.

"Muthafuckas say dat nigga J-Dawg up in there singin' like one of the Temptations," Paco said, breaking the silence and ending Troy's deep thought.

"Yeah, well, dat nigga been a bitch! I just hope he don't try to put my muthafuckin' name in that shit!" Troy responded, starting the engine as one of his runners approached the van.

"We need to go get another bundle," Troy said to Paco as the runner climbed in through the side door and immediately began counting the money he'd collected.

———⦾⦾⦾———

Bells and alarms all went off at the same time in Troy's head as he approached Renee's block and saw the ambulance and police cars everywhere. Unable to get through the congested street cluttered by police cars and nibby neighbors, he took to foot prying his way through to the focal point of everyone's curiosity. His heart nearly stopped as he saw two policemen rolling a stretcher with a body bag on it out of Renee's front door and placed it on the back of the coroner's van. Refusing to be restrained, he propelled beyond the human barricade set by the police and made it to the porch in time to see another body bag being brought out.

"*Renee!*" he screamed as a few uniforms restricted his entrance into the house.

"My son is in there!" he yelled, struggling to free himself of their hold.

"Please calm down, sir. No one else was in the residence," a plainclothes officer said as he approached, peeling latex gloves from his hands.

Troy could hear nothing beyond physical denial of entrance already in progress as he fought to be admitted.

"Sir, what is your relation to the victims?" The plainclothes spoke, sounding like he was under water to Troy, while everything around him slowed to a snail's pace.

Troy dropped to his knees in a defeated posture, still not hearing the plainclothes officer's words, sobbing into his hands.

"Sir, what is your relation to the victims?" he repeated.

"My son lives here with his mother and grandparents," he finally replied.

"There were no children in the residence. The two victims were elderly. Do you have a contact number for your son's mom?" asked the detective.

"Yeah," Troy responded, pulling his phone from his pocket, and placing the call to Renee's phone.

Not even thirty seconds later, another police officer stepped out of the house onto the front porch, holding up the ringing phone to the detective standing next to Troy.

"Maybe she and the kid stepped out for a minute, and she forgot the damn thing," one of the other uniforms said to no one in particular.

But Troy knew differently. He knew that Renee and her phone were fused together. Wherever she went, her phone went. Something was wrong—something was terribly wrong.

After being interviewed by the police, Troy rode around, trying to calm his nerves and make sense of things. He was both nervous and angry that he couldn't reach Renee with his son. *How could this bitch leave her damn phone today of all days?* he thought angrily to himself as he drove on.

And then his phone rang.

CHAPTER 41

"YO!"

"Troy!" Renee screamed into the phone.

"Renee, where the fuck—"

"If you want to see this bitch and the kid alive again, chu do what I say!" a voice interrupted and ended just as abruptly. Then the phone went dead with a click.

After the call, Troy was enfeebled—torn by the very thought of his son being in the hands of his worst enemy. The number was blocked, so he had no way of reconnecting the call and no choice but to wait and worry himself sick.

Day after day, he watched his cell phone, waiting for them to call with instructions that never came. He'd do anything to save his son, even if it meant losing his own life.

Over the next two days, he fell deep into a pitiful state, staying inside most of the day snorting the white powder god he'd once fallen in love with. Somewhere during that four-day period, he accepted the fact that he may never get to see his son alive again, and revenge became the driving force. He would not rest until he got that revenge—no matter the cost. He paid for the funeral services of Renee's parents but didn't attend because he felt their blood was on his hands, and he couldn't bear seeing them lying there because of him.

"Aye, I know how this probably sounds. But these niggas killin' you because they done took all you love. We gotta strike back and take what they love," Paco stated, hoping his words would be taken as a reflection of his concern and dedication to Troy.

"That's been my exact thought for the past day, Bro. I'm ready to say fuck everything and go all out! Shit'd they got my lil man. And God forbid …" Unable to complete the sentence, his voice trailed off.

"What if they took Renee and shorty over to Colombia? You ever been over there with dat nigga, Bro?"

Troy began with a slow contemplated, "No," as the wheels of his cocaine-induced mind started turning, more like spinning. "Naw, I ain't never been over there. But I've seen pictures of the estate. I know what it looks like!" he finished with an epiphanous nod.

"I'm drawin' the same thing, bro, on everything. But how the fuck we gone get the burners and shit over there?"

"I ain't got that figured out yet. But first and foremost, we goin' over there to get that nigga's father and see what that nigga wanna do. If he acts like he don't wanna get right, then we gone get his mama and anybody else. I'm gonna go see my brother this weekend, cuz I gotta holler at him about something. Bet he know how we can get at these niggas!"

"Yeah, I thought that fool was 'bout to get out and shit. What's up with that?"

"He downtown, been back for about a year now, waiting on the judge to rule. They keep giving him these long-ass continuances cuz they 'on' wanna let a nigga go. Shit'd, he been gone ten years now and just getting his appeal granted."

"Aye, tell that crazy nigga I say what up and that we all out here pullin' for him and shit to come to the crib," Paco said, leaving to make the rounds to the blocks to check on the workers.

<hr />

"So, let me get this straight, young blood," the raspy voice began. "These niggas killed both of Renee's parents and took Renee and Lil Troy, and now you need me to convince Mama to go up to Aunt Geraldine's for a few to let this shitstorm you started blow over?" he said, slowly nodding his head as if he understood.

"Look, J. I got round-the-clock security on Mama. Everywhere she goes, I got Bros in place to make sure she's straight without her even knowin' it. I just need you to get her to go up to there while I finish getting at these niggas. Security is gonna still be right there with her."

"First off, if anything happens to Moms, you already know what it is, young blood. I'll talk to her and get her to go, but you betta clean this mess up! Call Joann tonight. She don't get off work until like around nine; she should be home by ten. Naw, on second thought, just go over there. And I'ma have her put you in touch with my man, Panama Jak. He can help you out with what you tryna do. He's my people, good dude," his brother said before getting up and walking out of the visiting room just as smooth as he had entered.

Panama Jak was an older Panamanian named Mario who Troy's brother, Jerry, had met over eight years ago at USP Pollock. They called him Panama Jak because that's where he was from. And his case dealt with robbing smugglers coming into the Port of Miami. He and Jerry had been cellmates for seven years before the big riot of 2000 over the terrible food and poor living conditions in the prison. Jerry had been transferred because the administration felt he was too influential over the prison population.

Panama Jak had been released a couple of years later but had stayed in contact with Jerry through his girlfriend, Joann. Jerry, or J-Rock as they called him in the penitentiary because of his affiliation with the Bros, and Panama Jak were like brothers. Their bond had been forged under the most hellacious circumstances any man could ever find himself in. To live in a six-foot-by-nine-foot cell with another man is the equivalent of living in a bathroom. You ate, slept, and shat in this tiny space. Most times, you weren't alone while engaging in any of these activities because of lockdowns. Respect was mandatory; camaraderie was a cherished blessing. Friendships formed in situations such as this proved to be stronger and to last longer than others because loyalty was so important in this concrete jungle, where cowardice camouflaged as courage paraded amid numbers until checked or challenged, and truly only the strongest survived.

J-Rock was well respected on the yard. He was a no-nonsense, stand-up guy with a real sense of fair play. When Mario came to the prison, it was predominately black, with a sprinkle of whites and less than a handful of Hispanics. J-Rock's old cellmate had gone home the week before, and he had the only open cell on the range. So, the CO had asked if he'd let the new inmate sleep there for a few nights until the counselor came into work on Monday.

The blacks didn't have a problem with it, but the Sureños were serious about their own only living with their own kind—so much that they would state they'd have to go to segregation before living with a black. Mario strongly disagreed with this because he knew the heritage of his people—that they were of black descent. When the Sureños tried to force Mario to go to segregation, J-Rock stood up for him. And the blacks stood up with J-Rock, turning it into a black-versus-brown issue. The blacks outnumbered the browns by at least seven to one. So needless to say, Mario went into J-Rock's cell that night and remained there, living with a black until J-Rock was transferred.

After that incident, they had become tight. And over the next few years, their bond had grown, and they'd become like brothers. They worked out together, lifting weights five days a week. And on the weekends, they took turns cooking the meal for the special institutional movies shown each week. Mario wasn't really the movie type, but he looked forward to watching them as part of the weekly routine that made his time go by faster. At night, they told stories of their lives, the places they'd been, and the things they'd seen and done.

J-Rock told the story of a hard life growing up in the projects, not having enough to eat, snatching purses, and robbing to help bring money into the house. He and several of his friends from the Dearborn Housing Complex where they lived had banded together with the Bros to stop the dudes from the neighboring projects from coming over and robbing or mugging them and their families. He talked about how he'd been in and out of juvenile detention centers since he was eleven years old and had then received a life sentence from the feds at the age of thirty.

Mario's story was one of hard work, struggle, and loss. He'd lived in Panama until he was twelve years old when his mom died from influenza, and his father had sent him and his little brother to live with relatives here in the States—relatives who didn't want them. The boys spent many nights on the streets, homeless and hungry after being discarded by their relatives like useless bubblegum wrappers. When they were lucky, they got to stay in the bus station, which was about two days out of the week when the brutish security guard that always chased them away wasn't working. Some nights, they found refuge and shelter in the hallways of buildings with unlocked doors.

One night while in the bus station, they were approached by a man who promised to give them a hundred dollars each to retrieve a bag from a locker in the station and bring it to him. Mario didn't know what the contents of the bag might be and didn't care. The promise of the money and thoughts of what could be bought held more importance than all else.

When they handed the bag over to the man waiting outside, he in turn handed them two crisp hundred-dollar bills. What happened next changed their lives forever.

The man went into cardiac arrest. Mario sent his little brother, Topo, to get help. When the man woke up three days later, Mario and Topo sat before him clenching the black bag they'd retrieved from the locker at the station.

The man was a loner and had no family, no wife, or children, and didn't believe in being attached to anything anyone could use to hurt him. He trusted no one beyond the scope of his control and never left anything to chance. However, something about the two little boys made him go against that rule, and he took them in and raised them.

Life was different for little Mario and Topo after going home with the man. The man's name was Bin, he was Iranian. His housekeeper, Rose Marie, cared for the boys when he was away on business. She taught them to read, write, and do arithmetic. He taught them hand-to-hand combat and to fish and hunt, along with swimming and all the things of survival that came with being a man.

Mario was sixteen when he'd found out what Bin actually did for a living. Early one morning, he hid in the back of Bin's work truck under the tarp he covered it with just before he left for an "out-of-town assignment," as he often called them. Mario went unnoticed for the two hundred plus miles. When Bin discovered his presence, he'd already taken the shot that had neutralized his target. It was too late for anything but to either neutralize the kid and continue his escape or include him in that escape. He chose the latter.

Bin had been livid! He'd cursed repeatedly in his native language for most of the drive. In his early years, the decision to kill the kid would have been an easy one without a second thought. Now there was only one thing to do; he would explain the nature of his occupation to the boy. He kept questioning himself. Had he become too careless in his old age? There was a time when he could have detected the change in the weight of the load he carried just by the feel of the truck. The kid weighed at least a one 155 pounds, he thought to himself. How could he have not known the difference? he pondered.

Luckily, the harsh realities of life had already done their work on young Mario, and he was unfazed by what he'd witnessed. He took the revelation of Bin's dealings without the slightest flinch. From that day forward, the two shared a different relationship, one where Bin began teaching him to hunt not only beast but also man.

After Bin's death, Mario and Topo returned to Panama, seeking their biological father and family, only to find their father sick and dying. Their country was still struggling to recover from the damages done by the past tyrant rulers of Colombia. The Noriega situation with the United States was being handled behind the scenes, to be swept under the rug.

Mario had returned to the states, while Topo had chosen to stay in Colombia and fight alongside his countrymen for a better Panama.

CHAPTER 42

"PAPI!" ELISE SAID, dropping her purse at the living room's entrance just as she came through the front door.

"Lisa baby, what are you doing here? I told you, I'm fine. You shouldn't have come all this way to see about me. Those young punks didn't do nothing to me. I'm old school, baby girl; it's going to take more than what they got to hurt me. And who is this beautiful woman you've brought with you?"

"Papi, I've come to take you away from here. Edwardo is now involved, and things are gonna get ugly fast. If they cannot get to Antonio, they'll come for you again. That's the way it goes, Papi!" She stressed her warning, ignoring his arrogant bravado and questions as to who Maria was.

"I don't need to go anywhere, baby girl. I have told you, these ain't nothing but punks! Let them come back, and I'm going to put some hurry up on their asses!" he said, revealing the 9 mm he had concealed under the blanket that covered his legs where he sat on the couch.

"Tu Eres terco!" She stormed off with her housemaid Maria in tow. "Las Maletas vamonos!" she called to her over her shoulder.

"Speak English in my house, young lady. You know I can't understand you when you start rolling your tongue and shaking that head of yours like your mother," he teased her.

"You are so stubborn, Papi, ugh!" she said as she and Maria continued up the stairs.

"You may as well get up because you're coming with me when I get back downstairs!" she went on. Elise was passionate like her mother when she made her mind up to do something. That was one of the things about her mom that had made him fall in love with her—her passion. When she'd set her heart and mind to do something, there was nothing on this side of heaven that could stop her. Elise had that same spirit about her and had used it to get what she wanted her entire life. Sadly, though, it was that trait that had come to be the main reason he and her mom had split years ago. She was so passionate and headstrong, never willing to compromise and too often becoming physical with him.

Returning with his things packed, she instructed Maria to take them out to the car and put them in the trunk.

"Look, Papito, you know I am not leaving here without you. So, we can do this the easy way or the hard way. Don't make me call Edwardo and have him send over his guardaespaldas, cuz you know I will. And they will pick you up and move you where I say. Come on, Papi. Why you gotta be so difficult?"

"This is my home, Lisa, and I'm not letting no little punks run me off! These little snot-nosed gangbangers don't scare me. I live or die here, baby. I'm sorry, but that's just the way it is!"

"Tell you what," Troy said, stepping into view and revealing Maria held by one of his men with a gun to her head. "You can either get ya old ass up and come with me, or you can get dead right here like you said!" He pointed his gun at both the older man and Elise.

"We ain't going' nowhere with you lil niggas. So do what you gotta do, chump!" the old man said through clenched teeth.

Boom! Without warning, the one holding Maria pulled the trigger, blowing her brains out of the side of her head and onto the wall.

"*Nooo!*" Elise screamed out as Maria's lifeless body sank to the floor like a sandbag into the ocean, and the killer quickly moved around the coffee table and seized her.

"*Papi!*" she screamed again as he yanked her to her feet, away from her father's side where she'd cowered.

"Don't try to be no fuckin hero, Papa!" Troy said, pulling back the hammer of the .40 caliber Glock he aimed at him.

Seeing Maria lying motionless in a puddle of her own blood and knowing Elise's life now hung in the balance of his next decision, he released his grip from the 9 mm trained on Troy under the blanket.

"That's more like it, Pops." Troy said when he saw the old man's hands come from under the cover empty. "Now get the fuck up and over here before my man here gets trigga-happy again and push her shit back too!"

"Just don't hurt her. She has nothing to do with this! Whatever you want, just take me and leave her out of this."

"I don't want your daughter, Pops. She's pretty, but I just ain't been able to think about pussy these days, since your bitch-ass son and son-in-law snatched my son and his mommy. Naw, I didn't come for no pussy. The two of you are gonna help me get my people back!" Troy stated.

They rushed Elise and her father out the back door and into the waiting black van parked in the alley behind the house. The trip was short, somewhere in the neighborhood, her father thought for sure. He sat beside his daughter, cloaked in the darkness provided by the knapsacks over their heads.

"Call him!" Troy demanded, handing Elise a cell phone after removing the knapsack from her head.

She dialed the number she had been given for Edwardo when she'd landed in Miami yesterday but got no answer.

"You'd better get somebody on that fuckin' line, lil mama, cuz time is running out for you and ole Papito here!" he warned.

This time, she tried Tony's number, and he picked up on the third ring. "Antonio, estoy en una bodega—"

"I'll take it from here!" Troy cut in, taking the pone from Elise. "What's up, bro? Seems like it's been forever since I last seen yo bitch ass. No need for you to talk, so don't say shit! I got the floor this time, and I'm making the fuckin rules! You see, I just couldn't get on board with me comin' to you and trustin' you to let my son and his mama go, so I went got yo pops and sista—you know, to even shit up a bit. So now I got yours like you got mines," he said and ended the call.

"Get your filthy hands off me, *hijo deputa*!" Elise squirmed as one of Troy's men groped her breast from behind the chair, she sat cuffed to.

"Shut up, bitch. You know you like it! You want some of this 100 percent grade A black dick, bitch," he said, licking her on the neck.

"Coma mieta!" she said and spat on the floor to her side.

"Aye cut that shit out, nigga. We ain't got time for that. Matter of fact, listen up, everybody. Don't nobody touch this bitch. She's off limits until further notice!" Troy ordered. "Don't you worry, sunshine. Edwardo and Antonio had betta come correct, or gettin fucked is gonna be the least of your worries. I promise. You and Papa here are gonna get dead quick if I don't get my fuckin son back!" he warned, holding her by the face with one hand squeezing her jaw.

CHAPTER 43

"SO, THE RETURN to the Game Tour, you're going to be sharing the stage with Jak Tha Rippa and Last Born Entertainment. How sick is that going to be?"

"Yeah, it's gonna be off the chain out there! Jak Tha Rippa and Last Born is my man n'em. they bring great energy, and his passion for the music takes it to another level whenever he's a part of the lineup. It's gonna be wild out there, so get them tickets!"

"And you've brought gifts I understand for our entire 106 & Park audience, right?"

"Oh, no doubt. We got my new CD for everyone and tickets for a few lucky guests to the show tonight here in New York!"

"That's right. D-Boy's got the hookup for five lucky audience members if they can correctly answer five questions about D-Boy's last album, *The Life of a Playa*, right, D-Boy?"

"That's right free, plus limo service and backstage passes for photos."

"OK, that's what's up! We're gone hop back into this crazy countdown and go to the next video. Coming in at number one for the third week is 'Girls, Girls, Girls.'"

Pretty changed the channel, disgusted by the sight of Danny, and

Stank. It was like they were getting away scot-free with murder—all on TV and touring the country as if they'd done nothing wrong. Meanwhile she was living in seclusion like a rat in witness protection. She knew Bang had done many things and crossed a lot of people. She understood what could come with the game he was into and even how it could affect her just being with him. But what she could neither understand nor get over was the fact that Danny had tried to kill her. She'd sucked him, fucked him, hell he'd even fucked her in the ass. But what part of the game was this where he'd try to kill her?

She felt pains associated with the wounds he'd caused, the aching disfigurement she'd fought to overcome through rehabilitation and therapy. She was still beautiful to most, but she would never see herself that way again with the scars of betrayal she wore upon her heart and skin. She'd been forced to leave the city she grew up in and loved, the only home she'd ever known—chased away from her mother, family, and friends, most of whom knew her to be dead. The unspeakable pains were those caused by loneliness and fear, abandonment, and worthlessness, as if her life meant nothing, even to God.

She searched for solace but found none—not in the stores and malls, not in the arms of men, not in the lecture halls of the university, and not even in the huddle of her clique of thieves. Only revenge and payback would grant her the peace and strength she needed to face tomorrow with the confidence to believe in herself again. *But how?* she thought as she continued channel surfing.

Her cell rang, breaking into her thoughts. She tossed the remote onto the couch beside her in exchange for the phone.

"Hey, Steph. What are you up to?" asked Jenny as soon as she answered.

"Gurl, nothing, sitting her flipping through these channels."

"Come out with me to a fundraiser for George Bush."

"I'ma black woman, boo boo. I don't do the Bushes! You do know Jessie told us to Stay out of the Bushes, don't you?" Pretty said with a laugh.

"Come on, Steph. It's for a good cause. Plus, we get exposure for the Kute Kittens Foundation in a larger arena. Besides, it's not even election year, and I ain't voting for him either if he does decide to run for a second term. Gurl Please! I'm not some dumb white girl here, sister!"

All Pretty could do was laugh and agree to go with her. "Who else is going, sista girl?"

"Sharon's going also. Well actually it's Sharon who we're going with. Her uncle's the one holding the event. He's a staunch Bush supporter!"

"Wait a minute—a black Republican? Are you bullshittin' me, gurl?"

"Nope! Sharon says he even goes wild turkey hunting or something with Dick Chaney every November. She calls him Uncle Phil, like on *The Fresh Prince of Bel-Air*."

"Well, I guess since it's for a good cause and all, that being the Kute Kittens Charity Foundation, count me in," Pretty said, giving a sarcastic meow.

After ending the call, she reclaimed the remote from beside her and paused at the sight of the detective from Chicago who'd come to see her in the hospital after the shooting. He and his partner had tried to get her to remember anything about the shooting she could that would help with the investigation, but she declined, claiming she could remember nothing. She sat there watching him and his partner walking through another crime scene somewhere in Chicago covered by WGN News Network.

She unmuted the TV just in time to hear the reporter saying that the city had been named the murder capital after more than eighty murders in less than the first six months of the year. She recognized the area where they were at without the news even mentioning it. It was her neighborhood! She just sat there staring at the TV, hearing and not hearing what was being said. Then it hit her like a bat upside the head.

She bolted from the couch and headed into her bedroom closet where she kept her diary and keepsakes from home. "Here it is," she mumbled to herself, pulling out the card Detective Jason Brown had given her in case she remembers anything.

"Detective Jason Brown, Gang Crimes, I think I just remembered something that's gonna be very helpful finding Kevin Brown's murders," she said in a thoughtful voice. A sly smile crept across her face as she continued looking at the card.

CHAPTER 44

"HEY, BRO, DID you sleep well last night, cuz I slept like a baby!" Troy said when Tony answered the phone the next morning. "Now be a good little bitch like the dick suckin' flunky you are and put your boss Edwardo on!"

"Ah the big man with the giant huevos that has taken my money and now threatens to kill my wife. I don't care for these things. My wife I love very much, but respect—" Edwardo began.

"Nigga, save the commercial. I ain't hearing none of that shit! I'll push this bitch wig back for real, and Tony knows it! Now this is how it's gonna go down. There's an old, abandoned warehouse on 32nd and Drexel in the middle of the block. Be there in an hour, and don't try nothing stupid! The clock is tickin', nigga—*ticktock* muthafucka. Don't be late!"

Troy ended the call and paced the catwalk on the second level of the old ice cream factory where he held Elise and her father handcuffed in one of the offices. He didn't know how things would turn out. He'd done everything he could think of to maintain the upper hand in the exchange. *Fifty-seven minutes until showtime*, he thought as he clutched the Mini-14 and looked down over the rail where his men were gathered.

Red beams danced on the floor and along the concrete walls of the factory from the weaponry his men commanded. Panama Jak had really come through. He'd set Troy up nicely with pairs of AKs, SKs, HKs, ARs, Mini-14s, and fully automatic 9 mms with extended clips. Four of his dogs were lose on the prowl, sniffing and probing along the cracks and corners of the perimeter as if in search of something.

"Forty-two minutes!"

"Paco!" Troy spoke through the walkie-talkie, in the past, they'd been used by his street soldiers on the block to communicate. Today, they would be used to coordinate their efforts to get his son back.

"What's up, bro?" came the reply.

"Send Skinnie and Chris out to watch the front and back. Tell 'em to keep their eyes open and to stay on channel seven."

———————

The room was stale and dusty. An old desk sat, lonely, near the center of the back wall flanked by two old file cabinets rusting on either side from the bottom to the top of the last drawer. Empty crack vials and alcoholic beverage bottles littered the floor, competing for real estate. Elise sat handcuffed to her father on one side, and a worn out office chair with metal armrests and a rotted-out seat cushion on the other. The large picture window looking out into the factory was clouded with thick dust and grime. She could hear footsteps moving back and forth nearby, probably just someone pacing, she thought, and kept watch over her father where he sat, unconscious but still breathing.

Every few minutes, she checked for a pulse at his wrist that was cuffed to hers. They'd roughed him up pretty bad this time. She could see from the way it sat off to the side of his face that his nose was most likely broken.

She heard voices in the distance and the occasional barking from two or more dogs. She tasted blood that dried in the crack of her mouth from the backhanded slap she'd received when she told Troy she hoped his son was already dead and that he'd be joining him soon. The office door swung open, shining light into the dark, musky room that temporarily blinded Elise and gave the figure standing in the threshold a shadowy, mysterious appearance.

"Almost show time, Chica. Rise and shine. The party's 'bout to begin!" Troy said as he stepped in. "Stay!" he commanded the two enormous pit bulls that swaggered in behind him.

He pulled a key from the top pocket of the hunter's vest he wore and began uncuffing them from one another and re-cuffing their hands behind their backs.

"Seventeen minutes!"

"Got three Suburbans rollin' in from the west," a voice cracked in through the walkie-talkie.

"Aye yo, two Explorers comin up from the south," came another staticky voice, the tone excited.

"Showtime!" Troy barked. "You, you, and you, the three of y'all get up there on the second floor and spread out up there. Keep your eyes open and ya fingas on them triggas. Aim for the head, my niggas! Head shots only; they gone be wearin vests, so fuck the chest! *Go!*" he shouted, setting his men in place to attack if things went bad.

He, Paco and another of his most trusted stood in the center of the cavernous warehouse as the Colombians drove through the large delivery garage door. Skinnie and Chris followed behind the two Explores and took position with choppers at the ready.

Edwardo and Tony stepped out of the rear doors of the second truck after Edwardo's men.

"Where's my son?" Troy's voice boomed through the tense silence.

"Where's my wife?" Edwardo countered.

Troy turned his head and nodded, signaling two of his men, who emerged from the shadows holding Elise and her father at gunpoint.

"Now where's my son?"

Edwardo raised his right hand and motioned to the first truck. The rear door opened, and one of his men stepped out with Renee and TJ under gunpoint as well.

"Only one way to do this shit, nigga. Same time!" Troy stated.

Edwardo merely nodded in agreement.

As they began releasing their hostages, something shattered one of the side windows of the factory, hitting the concrete floor with a loud *clang*, and smoke began filling the building.

"Freeze! DEA. Put down your weapons now!" came a loud voice as federal agents began storming the premises by twos, looking like aliens in their goggled gas masks and riot gear.

"Rock, Zeus, hit!" Troy commanded, sending two of his pit bulls to attack as he attempted to escape with his son tucked into his chest.

The first shot went off, followed by a defeated yelp from one of the dogs, and then heavy gunfire erupted.

Troy's men rained down bullets on both Edwardo's men and the federal agents without prejudice. The fully automatic HK's bullets marched swiftly without repentance, finding their way into any available object of reception below. Three of Edwardo's men and two agents lay dead before the air raid was brought to a halt when agents took aim and killed the three above.

Moments later, silence fell upon the factory. The smoke continued its ride through the air like a surfer on the waves of a California beach, blanketing bodies of the dead and wounded where they lay.

Experience and training had certainly won this battle. Agents carefully swept through the area confiscating weapons from the dead, still caressing the triggers of their guns and assault rifles as they stared out into oblivion. Those found alive were taken into custody without resistance or further incident.

Tony lay riddled with bullets and stranded, alone and unable to move. Tears streamed from his face into a puddle of his own blood, where he lay terrified at the thought of dying there alone on the cold concrete floor. His life played out in his mind before him, beginning back when he was seven years old, and he'd intentionally hit his sister in the face with the football. Then it was the bicycle he'd taken from the little white kid. And on it went, scene after scene of every evil thing he'd done his entire life. He sobbed uncontrollably, face down in the growing puddle of blood, praying that whatever god existed would forgive him before he stood face-to-face with him.

Elise crawled along the cement floor, half dragging her wounded leg where she'd been shot. She couldn't find Edwardo and feared the worst. She heard sobbing and moved toward the sounds, finding her brother facedown and badly wounded, his body riddled with bullet holes.

"Antonio," she said in an urgent whisper.

"Elise, I can't move. I can't feel my body!" He began to panic.

"Shhh!" She hushed him, looking around and attempting to locate the sounds of the footsteps she'd just heard.

When she got close enough, she rolled him over onto her lap and placed his head in her lap. She stroked his face as she cried, telling him how much she loved him. The footsteps passed, and she continued telling her brother of her love and how everything would be all right just like always.

She knew what she had to do, as it would not be all right this time. The wounds to Antonio's back revealed his spine; and with the amount of blood he'd lost, he probably wouldn't last through the night. Even if he could survive, his heart had already been compromised. She continued stroking his face, praying with him, and then, in one swift motion, she twisted his head as hard as she could, snapping his neck and killing him instantly.

She cried while still stroking his face for a few moments more before screaming for help.

Agents cautiously approached the area the screams for help came from, guns trained on all before them. They moved in a side-to-side sweeping motion, following their eyes, ready to neutralize any threat to their squadron. They found Elise sitting on the ground cradling Tony's head in her lap, his lifeless body stretched out between her legs.

One of the agents kicked the weapon away from Tony's reach and kneeled to check for signs of life.

"He's gone, ma'am. I'm going to need you to come with us, ma'am!" one of the agents said in a muffled tone through his mask.

At first, the brilliant afternoon sun was blinding to Elise's already irritated eyes as the two agents helped her out of the dark, dingy, smoke-filled factory and in two one of the waiting ambulances.

"I'm Special Agent Johnston with the DEA, Mrs. Comez. I have a few questions for you," said the white woman who appeared at the rear of the ambulance while the paramedics attended to Elise's leg wound.

Elise was noticeably caught off guard. What had Tony told the Feds about her? She tried to figure quicker than her mind would allow, causing her to display a dumbfounded look at the mention of her name. She knew of her brother's cooperation with the government, even of the plan to take down Edwardo. Her sources had informed her of as much, but had they neglected to tell her everything, it seemed. Was she, in fact, a part of the investigation? Was her and Danny's relationship known? And if so, to what extent? She sat perplexed, unable to disguise the discombobulation.

"Your father's neighbor reported what she thought to be a kidnapping when she saw you and your father being forced into a black van in the alley behind his residence two days ago. Says she became suspicious after hearing what sounded like a gunshot inside the house prior to the two of you being brought out at gun point," she said, reading from a pocket-sized notepad.

"My father!" Elise said, moving to get off the ambulance where she sat being attended to, remembering he was inside the factory.

"Your father is fine, Mrs. Comez. He was taken to Michael Reese Medical Center to have tests run. He's not alone. I have two agents stationed outside his door. I'm sorry about your brother. He went dark about a month or so ago. He stopped taking my calls, started avoiding me. I wanted to bring him in, in the States. We had to see where it would lead us."

"What? My brother?" Elise looked confused, as if she had no idea about what the agent was talking about.

"Your brother was working to help bring your husband and the Dominguez Cartel to justice. You're not in any trouble, Mrs. Comez. But you do need to talk to us because, when Edwardo finds out that your brother has been working with the government to bring him to justice, neither you nor your parents will be safe. You gotta be smart here, Elise. We can have your mother brought to the States with just one phone call."

"What is it that you people think I can help you with? What do you think I know?" Elise responded, before being interrupted before Agent Johnston's radio.

"SA Johnston, over!"

"Go for Johnston!" she responded into her radio.

"We have a visual on the suspect at 35th and King."

"OK, stay with him. And remember the little package he has with him! I'm on my way."

"Agent Jones, Agent Wallace, take her to Michael Reese where her father is. And stay with her until I get there," she instructed the two agents.

"Make up your mind, Elise. Time is running out. I will join you at the hospital when I can. My men will stay with you and your father," she said before rushing off with another agent in tow.

CHAPTER 45

TROY DUCKED OUT the back door, continuing his escape, his son clinging to him like a baby koala bear to its mother. *That was close! Where the fuck did them muthafuckas come from?* he thought as he slowed down a few blocks away, attempting to blend in with the scenery. It was early March, and the kids were out playing under the watchful eyes of their parents. His goal was to look like a father out with his young son for an afternoon stroll. The only problem with that was TJ wasn't dressed for early March in Chicago. The temperature was a balmy thirty-five degrees, and everyone, including him at least, had on jackets. They passed by a few old women who just stopped and shook their heads at the sight of the little one underdressed for the cool weather.

He'd tried to flag down a cab a few times along the way. But it was a fruitless effort in this area because of all the stickup murders of cab drivers. Even with a small child, it was hopeless, as children were often used as a ploy to gain victims' trust of the victims.

Nosy ass old bitches! he thought, glancing back at the old ladies, who were still looking in his direction. He picked up his son and, once again, hurried along.

He made it to 35th and King Drive and saw the Foot Locker on the corner in the strip mall. He would go in and buy TJ a jacket and hat before continuing the careful trek to his mother's house on 29th.

"There you go, lil man," he said, zipping up his son's jacket and pulling his skully down over his cold little ears, preparing to continue their journey to safety.

"Freeze! DEA. Hands in the air. Get on the fucking ground!" he heard as they stepped out into the midday air.

He looked down at his son clinging to his leg terrified and knew it was over right then and there. He bent down and kissed TJ on the top of his head and gently shoved him away before raising the Mini-14 he'd concealed under his jacket.

Everything went silent for little Troy as he saw the fire escaping the guns of the policemen and his father falling in slow motion to the ground.

———❖———

"Edwardo was nowhere in the factory, Mrs. Comez. My men swept the entire building. He must have somehow escaped during the commotion," Special Agent Johnston said after rolling Elise outside her father's hospital room.

Toggling between being relieved and distraught, Elise breathed a crestfallen sigh and sunk deeper into the wheelchair for greater effect.

"He's more than likely attempting to leave the country, heading back to Colombia as we speak. I can protect you and your family, Mrs. Comez, but my hands are tied. It's up to you. Do the smart thing here before it's too late."

Elise sat there for a moment as if torn between her loyalty to the man she loved and her family. Regardless of what she knew to be true about Edwardo, he was a man facing serious drama. And there was no telling what he was capable of at this point. Survival of the family was of the greatest importance, and everyone had their part to play. Tony had played his part. Now it was time for Edwardo to play the role he was cast for, even if he wasn't aware of just what that role would entail.

She sat for a moment longer, pretending to wrestle with herself over the tough decision. Finally, after what appeared to be deep contemplation, she looked up at the agent and agreed to cooperate with them.

"Where do I start? What do I need to do?"

CHAPTER 46

J-ROCK SAT STONE-FACED on the back of the truck as it made its way over the rocky terrain, bouncing at every dip and bump and causing him to sway from side to side. He'd only been out a week. His little brother had been gunned down nearly a month ago. His mother had suffered a massive stroke after hearing of her youngest child's death and lay in a coma. Nothing could keep him away from the instigator of his current sorrows in life.

His man, Panama Jak, sat across from him with a deathly serious face as he loaded the 7.62 caliber SKS—just one of the many weapons they'd purchased from the little old arms dealer his brother, Topo, had set them up with before leaving Coclé. Neither of the men spoke; words were not necessary, for revenge was the catchy instrumental of death that had played so often throughout their entire lives that they'd come to know its tune by heart.

The boat ride over from Coclé to Colombia was maybe an hour, an hour-fifteen. During the ride, Topo explained the layout of the estate and what obstacles they would face getting there. He told of the bands of wild men living in the jungle that lay just outside Edwardo's compound about a mile away. He'd received intel from sources near the border that

189

the Dominguez Cartel was not well liked by the jungle people. Although the Colombians and Panamanians generally didn't like one another, this particular tribe of jungle people they would encounter was quite close to the border and traded with Panamanians almost daily.

"The enemy of my enemy is my friend!" Topo smiled as he nodded in the direction of Colombia sitting in the distance, referring to the jungle people moving about the shores.

"One hundred years of aggression my people endured from Colombia!" he said, sweeping his arm in a backward motion toward the three boats full of his men behind them. "Panama became an independent nation in 1903 after countless wars with Colombia. They wanted us to remain under their rule. But we are a strong people, and we cannot be suppressed!

"I'm sure Mario has told you how we were raised in the States. I returned when I was old enough to take my place alongside my people where I belong. Not so for Mario. He's a man of the world, an untamed spirit that must roam freely to and fro. I honor you, brother J-Rock. Because of him, I am alive today. Because he says that you have been like a brother to him, me and my men will fight with you until the death if it comes to that!" Topo steered the boat, looking out at the water before them.

The jungle people looked like something you'd see on *National Geographic*. The women ran around with their breasts exposed and hanging like it was nothing. The men wore tribal marking and piercings in their faces. They had a prehistoric look, but they were far from primitive. Their armory was that of a small militia. They had American, German, and even Russian weaponry in their possession. Topo spoke to the leader in Spanish, and he quickly welcomed the group into their cluster with a rotted smile and a welcoming pat on the back.

Topo turned back and mouthed, *the enemy of my enemy is my friend*, nodding confidently. They only needed to pass through the camp, but the leader was determined to send men with them to be sure they didn't run into any problems along the way. And you don't just turn down help from a tribal leader without insulting him and the tribe.

When they approached the estate, they saw it was large and spacious. There were no gun towers, which was good, Topo said, because the surprise element would prove to be helpful to them in their attack. A brick wall about seven feet tall stood around the property with cast iron gates at the entrance and near the rear. They took positions atop a small hill looking down into the grounds. J-Rock could see dogs on the loose and Edwardo's men patrolling with assault rifles that they would need to take out to enter at the rear.

Topo sent men to the far east side of the estate nearer to the back to see what things looked like there. They reported back that no activity was in the rear, which was a lucky surprise, he commented.

They would still need to take out the dogs and the men in the front in order to launch a successful attack from the rear. Four of Topo's men would strike from the hill above the estate, sniping out as many of the men on the compound as they could, while another band of his men stormed the front in a distracting attack to draw the attention of the remaining soldiers inside. Meanwhile he, Panama Jak, and J-Rock would come in through the back.

The three made their way over the wall and onto the grounds, flanked by Topo's eight remaining men. The back of the mansion was about forty yards from where they had entered, with a large swimming pool adjacent to its structure. They split into two groups and approached from either side, reconverging at the rear entrance of the building. In no time, they were inside, moving about in search of Edwardo.

Panama Jak's Mac 90 went off first as he caught one of Edwardo's men descending the staircase to the left of him, sending him tumbling down the stairs in slow motion like an overstuffed plastic bag of clothes. Next J-Rock caught movement in his peripheral to the right of them and opened fire, catching another of Edwardo's men on his way to deliver help to his comrades under fire outside.

One of Topo's men went down behind them, and they all took cover in response to the sound of rapid shots before returning fire and eliminating the threat. Another of Topo's men quickly made a tourniquet from the bandana around his head and applied it to the leg of his wounded friend as the others continued their raid. Gunfire from above caused them to scatter for cover behind a wall separating what appeared to be two living rooms.

"We need to split up and find a way to the upper level," Panama Jak suggested.

They separated into groups of two men. Topo, Panama Jak, and J-Rock opened fire on the shooters above to provide cover for the others to move from where they were pinned in. Moments after they were gone, the sounds of rapid fire from their machine guns could be heard above, followed by the body of another of Edwardo's men flying over the top rail and crashing to the marble floor below.

The trio made their way to the upper level to join the two squadrons they had dispersed minutes ago. Taking two steps at a time, J-Rock hurried to the top as Panama Jak and Topo covered him from the rear, slowly rotating in a near 360-degree motion one step at a time, carefully watching for any surprises that lay ahead or behind them.

The upper level of the structure was expansive with multiple bedrooms, bathrooms, and a library or study of some sort. There was a second living room, a dining room, and a fitness room that led out to a balcony. Topo noticed the exchange outside had died down and radioed his men to check the status. He was informed that his men had completely neutralized the forces they had faced but had spotted a convoy of about four trucks approaching from the east, about a mile and a half out. He quickly relayed the intel to his brother and J-Rock as they continued their search of the living quarters.

Edwardo lay holding a .45 automatic trained on the door as he heard footsteps approaching, unable to move. The wounds he had sustained in the firefight with the federal agents and Troy's men at the warehouse had all but taken his life. Had it not been for his little cousin Chio, who drug him out and got him to the safety of one of the vans they had on standby near the rear of the building, he would surely already be dead. From there, it had been touch-and-go with only limited supplies. It was nothing short of a miracle that his travel-along physician had been able to keep him alive until they made it to Miami. Now he lay recovering from the bullet wounds, facing certain death once more as the footsteps got closer.

Topo signaled that he heard movement in the room to their left, touching his ear and pointing in the direction of the door. J-Rock got the message and bent into a crouching stance at the side just before the door's frame. He checked the doorknob, and it was locked. He signaled for two of Topo's men to stand at both sides of the door and cover high while he went low.

Before the men could get into place, shots came through the door from inside the room, striking one of the men in the neck. With no time to waste, J-Rock shot the doorknob and plowed through with his shoulder from a squatting position. He rolled across the floor like something from *T. J. Hooker* or *Starsky & Hutch*.

Edwardo continued firing from his position on his back in the bed. The loud *click* of the pistol's empty chamber repeated a few times.

J-Rock rose with the assault rifle aimed at the figure that lay in the bed. It was Edwardo, he assumed, looking at the man who resembled Antonio Banderas playing Jesus.

"You killed my brother, you spick piece of shit!" he said, looking down at Edwardo.

"Your brother deserved to die. But I didn't kill him. The fucking feds killed your brother," he responded, any other words he might have said drowning in as he an uncontrollable fit of coughing.

"Come on, J-Rock. We gotta get out of here. No time for words," Panama Jak urged.

"Do what you will to me. I am already dead. My times is up regardless of what happens here today. I am no longer of any use," Edwardo said and laughed, setting off another coughing fit.

Without another word, J-Rock fired a single shot through Edwardo's forehead.

***

The ceremony for Tony was a small private affair with only family and the closest of friends in attendance. Elise sat hidden behind designer shades next to her mother as the procession of people passed by paying their respects to the deceased, stopping at them to offer condolences.

She had received word of Edwardo's death and had taken it with great happiness and relief. He had fulfilled the purposes for which she'd married him. She was a black widow, plotting, planning, and strategizing from the very beginning with her lover. Yes, it was her who'd convinced Edwardo to supply Antonio with multiple kilos each month—or, rather, she'd instructed him to do so. Nothing could have been done to save Antonio. He was weak and had no place in the family business. Edwardo had failed to carry out his orders to kill Tony when he was sent to Chicago. And, thus, his fate had been brought upon him in the fashion it had come.

Elise studied the woman claiming to carry Tony's child and wondered if the unborn fetus carried her traits or those of Antonio. Only time would tell, she concluded, as they were introduced by Danny. They briefly embraced, and Elise thought of how the woman might be helpful to the family.

"So nice to meet you—uh, Loretta, is that right?" she asked.

"Yes, it is, Loretta Kline. Nice meeting you too."

"Now don't be a stranger and make me hunt you down to find my niece or nephew," Elise said with a deadly serious smile.

"I would never do such a thing; I believe in family wholeheartedly!" Loretta responded.

"Good! Walk me out to the car, Danny. I wanna have a word with you. And Mom wants to see you as well," Elise said, placing a hand on Danny's forearm.

EPILOGUE

Traffic on the expressway was bumper to bumper heading north. Detective Brown hated the morning commute, which was why his shift didn't begin until two in the afternoon. Today, though, he was pleasantly content in the cluster of impatient honkers moving at a snail's pace. In fact, he was a bit happy as he patted out a tune on the steering wheel, singing along with the radio.

Today, he and his partner, KB, were on their way to O'Hare Airport to pick up an eyewitness to an unsolved murder that had taken place four years ago. At the time, the witness had been too traumatized by the horrific attack to remember anything. This was common in many cases when a person has suffered great shock or stress to his or her mental capacity. The shutting down of the memory linking the person to the event was a protection mechanism the mind used to prevent greater emotional distress.

Oftentimes, such victims or eyewitnesses never recaptured the memory of what they'd seen. This was one of the few times when the victim had. A week ago, Detective Brown had received a call from a young woman who'd been shot multiple times in an attack that had left her boyfriend dead in Crestwood, Illinois.

He remembered the case because he had been asked to help with the investigation, which, in and of itself, was unusual because he worked for the City of Chicago. His assistance had been requested by the chief of police for the City of Crestwood because of his knowledge of gang crimes and his reputation. Chicago was the hub for many of the gangs that flooded the surrounding suburbs, and no one knew the inner workings of their structures like Detective Brown.

When the spill of violence had blown back into the Windy City, Detective Brown had taken full control of the investigation. He'd interviewed the young lady following the shooting but had been unsuccessful in getting anything helpful to the case. Now, miraculously, not only had she remembered the details of that awful night back in 1998, but she also believed she even knew the identity of the assailants.

The case had been a shitstorm, blowing in dozens of casualties from the war that ensued between the two gangs following the shooting. The feds had been called in and had brought criminal charges against the Vikings. Several arrests of the Bros had been made, and those caught up in the sweep had been tried in State court. But the murder of Kevin Brown had never been solved.

JB had his speculations as to who had committed the homicide, but without anything concrete, they were just that—speculations. It had frustrated him to the point of drinking, which in turn had caused problems at home. The way the shooting happened was execution style, not something he would attribute to the Vikings. It wasn't that they were incapable of it; it just didn't fit the working profile he had on them. For one, the location of the crime was only secluded at certain times, and to siege the opportunity at any of those exact moments took patient surveillance and planning. Secondly, the reenactment of the crime done by the crime scene investigators had revealed the involvement of a second vehicle, which had cordoned off the victim, preventing escape. The SUV occupied by the victims was still in drive, indicating something other than the driver hitting the brakes had brought them to a stop. This was definitely a mob-style hit in his mind.

Oftentimes, when a hit as bodacious as this took place, it was an inside job to send a message for underlings to stay in line. The Bros were a smaller, more unified gang than the Vikings. According to his information, and a hit like this didn't fit their MO either.

Maybe their predecessors, the Chicago Boys, back in their day—they were a disciplined and serious enough group to organize and carry out something like this, he'd thought at the time. However, they were locked away in federal prison, and had been since the mid '80s when the feds had begun moving in, taking down gang chiefs.

He disagreed with this tactic strongly; he felt that removing the heads of the gangs would only create a disregard for the codes and laws the gangbangers were held to by their leaders. When you cut the proverbial head off the snake, another one—and, in some instances, multiple heads— would grow in its place. This would create deadly battles for power within the gangs, he'd ranted at the time. He thought it was best to leave the gang chiefs on the streets where they could control their foot soldiers and maintain a certain amount of order.

It had been just over six months since Tony's death, and life seemed to go on uninterrupted. Danny sat in his plush office at D-Boy Studios listening to CDs submitted to him by aspiring artists. It was amazing the number of demo tapes and CDs he received daily from people he came in contact with on the streets.

Many artists in his field no longer took the time to check out the new talent on the horizon after they'd reached his level of stardom. Danny was different, though. He was always on the hunt for new talent. He dreamed of building a Death Row Records with the longevity of "Bad Boy Records."

He had even begun working with his son, Lil Jay, on his writing skills and delivery of bars. He planned to introduce Lil Jay to the world on one of his songs and then feature him in the songs of other artists on his label.

The clothing line he'd launched with Trina, Esa Wear, was doing well since appearing on one of New York's hottest fashion shows. Revenues were projected at $2.7 million for the year. Trina no longer worked for Hewlett Packard. She ran Esa Wear's day-to-day operations. She'd brought her girlfriend Nee Nee on board as her assistant/hairstylist.

Trina was happy, without complaint, despite Danny's cheating ways. She knew he was a cheater. But he was also a good father and provider. And for those reasons she stayed down with him through all the little flings he had behind her back. His latest episode had been with Tony's sister, the "taco eating bitch" as she and Nee Nee referred to her.

He had no clue she knew about them; he never did. She knew about the condo on the Gold Coast on the North Side that he shared with her. She also knew about the strip mall he had interest in that was being built by her. Still, she kept this and all that she'd come to know about her unfaithful husband to herself. Meanwhile, she snatched and stacked all that she could, just as her mother had advised her.

<hr>

Danny continued listening to demo CDs up until around noon, when he had to prepare for a meeting. Stank had come into his office a little over thirty minutes ago to see what plans he had for the rest of the day. They often met up throughout the day to see what the other had planned.

"Dee, two detectives are out here wanting to see you," said the receptionist through the intercom sitting on Danny's desk.

"Wait a minute! He ain't even said he was available to see y'all," the receptionist protested as the plainclothes officers moved her out of the way and headed for Danny's office.

"That's fine, Jasmine," Danny said, holding up a hand to let her know everything was cool.

"Hey there, D-Boeeey. And look, KB, it's *big Stank* too!" Detective Brown said in an exaggerated tone, crossing his arms across his chest with his hat cocked to the side like he was in a rap video.

"What can I do for you, detectives?" Danny asked as he reclined in his seat behind his massive desk.

"Oh, you can start by standing and putting your hands behind your back! I have an arrest warrant for the both of you, for the murder of Kevin Brown and attempted murder of Stephanie Douglas. Now, you have the right to remain silent. Anything you say can and will be used against you in a court of law. You have the right to an attorney. If you cannot afford an attorney, one will be provided for you. Do you understand your rights?"

"I don't know no damn body named Kevin Brown or Stephanie Douglas. This is bullshit!" Danny protested.

"Jasmine, call my attorney Blaine Caplan. His number is in the book!"

"Oh you knew Bang, and I'm certain you know Pretty," the detective said as they placed the handcuffs on both Danny and Stank and escorted them out.

All Danny and Stank could do was look at each other in shock and bewilderment.